YOUNG
INFIELD
ROOKIE

CHARLES COOMBS

YOUNG INFIELD ROOKIE

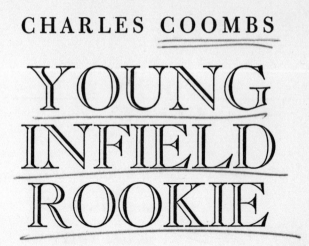

iC7744yo

ILLUSTRATED BY CHARLES H. GEER

LANTERN PRESS

NEW YORK

LIBRARY OF CONGRESS CATALOG NUMBER: 54-7281

PUBLISHED SIMULTANEOUSLY IN CANADA BY
GEORGE J. MC LEOD, LIMITED, TORONTO

MANUFACTURED IN THE UNITED STATES OF AMERICA

To the Little League players of today,
the nation's leaders of tomorrow.

CONTENTS

ILLUSTRATIONS

YOUNG
INFIELD
ROOKIE

CHAPTER ONE

"Zooming rockets, Ken," Bruno Prosser said, "don't be a chicken."

"Aw, Ken's not afraid," Grant Emerson spoke up quickly. "He—well—you're not afraid, are you, Ken?"

"Ken is all right," Corky Richards said. "You'll be there this afternoon, won't you?"

Ken Douglas looked at each of them. He had known this moment would come. Ever since he had read in the Brookdale *Star-News* about the Little League being formed again this year, he had known that they would be after him to play.

"There are plenty of fellows around here to make up four teams," Ken said. "Besides, I've got chores to do around the house and—and everything."

"We all have chores to do," Bruno said. He was short and husky and tanned a deep brown. His pug nose and firm wide jaw made him look almost tough. Last year Bruno had been catcher for the Brookdale Fire Department Red Sox. He planned to play the same Little League position again this season.

"I might even help you with your chores," Grant offered, then added, smiling, "but only once in a while." Grant was tall for his eleven years. He was blond-haired and wore glasses. He usually made a point of dressing in the oldest clothes he could get away with. The Emersons were quite well to do. They lived in a big house on a hill overlooking Brookdale. But Grant felt that was sometimes more of a handicap than a help. So he shied away from anything that made him appear more fortunate than his friends. He had been one of the star pitchers on the Red Sox roster last season.

"Even if I did try out," Ken said, "how do I know that I'd get to play with the Red Sox?"

"You don't know," Corky answered. "But if you're good enough, Captain McGrath might be willing to spend a lot of team credits to get you. When the players' auction comes up, I mean. The three of us got on the same team last year. We took that chance when we went out to make a team. You would just have to take a chance too."

"Maybe Ken doesn't like to take chances," Bruno said impatiently.

"What do you mean by that?" Ken challenged.

"I mean," Bruno said levelly, "that maybe you're just plain afraid that you will get hit with another ball like you did when we were playing sand-lot ball last spring."

"Take it easy, Bruno," Grant said quickly. "Ken's on our side."

"Maybe he is, and maybe he isn't," the

13

dark-haired boy retorted. "I'm not exactly sure we need a guy who's afraid to play base-ball just because he got hurt a little once."

Thoughts swirled wildly in Ken's mind. Bruno was pulling no punches. Now, instead of telling the stocky catcher to take it easy, both Grant and Corky looked at Ken. They seemed anxious to hear his answer. There had been a lot of little squabbles between the four of them during the years they had played together, but they didn't mean anything and were quickly forgotten.

Ken knew, though, that this argument was different. This one was much more serious. Bruno's point-blank accusation demanded a showdown.

Ken knotted his fists, although he had no intention of trying to use them on Bruno. Hot words rose in his throat, but he crowded them back. He crowded them back for one reason: Bruno might be right about him.

Perhaps he was afraid. Perhaps, too, he had a right to be afraid. Maybe Bruno would be even more afraid if he had known the pain of having his jaw broken by a hard-pitched wild ball. Would Bruno have found any joy in having his jawbone clamped together while it was mending? What did Bruno know about the ache and the hurt and the wild nightmares of other baseballs streaking toward his head, and not being able to get out of the way in time?

"O.K.," Ken said sharply, "I'm afraid. I— I'm a chicken. Now, if you're satisfied, why don't you beat it and leave me alone?"

It didn't seem to be the answer Bruno had expected. He glanced at Corky, then at Grant. He seemed uneasy. None of them found anything to say. It was one thing to suspect that their friend might be afraid to play baseball; it was quite another thing to have him suddenly admit it. Corky kicked at a small stone and sent it spinning out into the street. Grant tugged at his glasses and looked at the ground. Bruno looked toward Ken, yet not quite at him.

"Go on," Ken said hotly. "You found out

what you wanted to know. I'm scared. Plumb scared of my own shadow. Scram. I've got a lawn to mow."

"Look, Ken," Bruno began, "I didn't mean to. . . ."

"Beat it!" Ken yelled.

"Guess we better go," Grant said.

"Yeah," Corky agreed.

"See you around, pal," Bruno said.

The three of them turned and started walking away down the sidewalk.

"I hope you're satisfied," Ken yelled after them. Then he spun on his heel and headed toward the garage.

But the driveway swam before his eyes. He blinked rapidly to clear away the mistiness. Once inside the garage, he flopped down on the lid of an old storage trunk.

He just sat there, thinking—and trying not to notice the sick feeling in his stomach.

CHAPTER TWO

A week had gone by since the blowup between Ken and his three friends. Even though they often passed each other in the school hallways or sat in the same classrooms, there had been few words spoken between them.

On a couple afternoons Ken had ridden his bike past the Little League ball park. There he saw what must have been at least eighty boys tossing or batting balls around. Later, each team roster would be limited to fifteen players. That made sixty players in the four-team Brookdale Little League. So about twenty of the boys would not make the grade.

Most of them would swallow their disappointment and play in the minor league. They would be better prepared to earn a position on the major league the following season.

Ken didn't stop at the ball park, but rode on past each time. Yet there was an empty feeling inside him as he did it. He had really liked to play baseball. At least, up until the day of that wild pitch and his broken jaw. And, although the jaw had healed perfectly, something inside Ken had not.

It was Saturday morning. Ken was edging the front lawn along the sidewalk, when someone said, "Hiyah, Ken."

Ken looked up to see Amos Jackson coming along the walk. Amos was dressed in patched jeans. He wore a white T shirt that made his skin seem even blacker than ever. As usual, Amos was smiling. And, as usual, Ken found himself wishing he had teeth as white as the colored boy had.

"Hi, Amos." Ken straightened up and returned the smile. He noticed the baseman's glove dangling from Amos' belt. "Going down to the ball park?"

"I'm not out for Little League," Amos said simply.

"Why not?"

"Oh, I don't know," Amos said slowly. "Reckon I'm just not a good enough player, that's all. Not much sense in wastin' time, is there?"

"That's crazy," Ken argued. "You're a good player."

"Anyway, I reckon there are plenty of good players without me."

"I know what you mean," Ken said suspiciously. "You mean plenty of good players with whiter skins. Don't you?"

Amos merely smiled and shrugged.

"Boy, you are really nutty," Ken scolded. Yet, he knew of several times that Amos had been treated unkindly by some of the kids around Brookdale. Amos' father was a hard-working janitor around town. He kept several of the store buildings neat and clean. Yet, there were some shortsighted people around Brookdale who didn't seem to approve of the Negro family. Amos was one of eleven children.

"Hey," Amos said, changing the subject, "did you read in the paper about Lefty Gregory arriving home sometime today?"

"Lefty?"

"Yeah," Amos said, nodding. "Supposed to be coming in on the train. But I don't figure there will be any bands at the depot to meet him, do you?"

" 'Fraid not," Ken said. "Not after what the papers have been saying about him. Some guys sure have it tough. Lefty was Brookdale's hero when he went to the Cardinals' spring-training camp a couple of months ago. The first Brookdale player to get to the big leagues. And now. . . ."

"And now he's coming back a—a bum," Amos filled in. "At least, that's what a lot of people seem to think, even though they don't say it."

"Well, it's Lefty's problem," Ken said.

"He's the one who decided to quit baseball. And right when the Cardinals were counting on him as their prize rookie pitcher."

"Maybe you're right, Ken," Amos said, "but I thought maybe you and I could go down to the depot and watch him come in."

"Why?" Ken asked. He wondered if he really felt at all sorry for Lefty Gregory. After all, when a fellow bean balls one of his own teammates hard enough to put him into a hospital—well, Ken certainly didn't hold any soft spot in his heart for Randy Simmons. It had been Randy's wild pitch that had broken his jaw.

"No big reason, I guess," Amos said. "I just thought it might help keep him from feeling too lonesome. I don't like to see anyone feeling lonesome. Come on. At least, it will be fun watching the trains come in."

"Oh, all right," Ken said. "Only I better finish edging this lawn first."

"I'll sweep up after you," Amos offered, picking up the broom.

They arrived at the Brookdale depot a half

hour later. The station was a small peak-roofed building, smoky gray in color. Connected to one side of it was a tin-roofed freight shed. A wooden plank platform stretched beside the tracks about fifty yards in both directions from the station.

Mr. Perkins, the station agent, smiled out at them from behind the grilled ticket window.

"Nope," he said, "Gregory didn't arrive on the eight-forty-five train. Might be he'll get in on the eleven-fifteen. You're the first ones who have asked."

Ken glanced at the wall clock behind Mr. Perkins. It was two minutes after eleven.

"We'll wait and see, huh, Ken?" Amos said.

"Might's well, I guess," Ken said. "Thanks, Mr. Perkins."

"Hope you boys aren't here to razz Lefty when he gets off," the station agent said, looking at them closely. "That lad has had plenty of trouble already."

"Razz him?" Ken said. "Oh, but we

wouldn't do that, Mr. Perkins. No, sir."

"If he's not on the eleven-fifteen, he may not figure on getting in until tonight," the railroad man said. "Might be he's even planning on it."

"We'll see," Amos said.

The two boys climbed up and sat on the bed of an empty luggage cart. It was only a few minutes until the whoo-oo-ee of a train whistle reached thier ears from the eastern outskirts of town. Then the plume of smoke was visible over the trees. A minute later the locomotive came chuffing around a distant bend in the tracks.

Then the black engine was slowing down for the stop. As it passed the two boys, they heard the rumble of fire in the great boiler. They pointed and laughed as a giant ring of black smoke coughed up from the stack. Just beyond them the engine came to a sighing stop, jets of steam hissing from its cylinder cocks.

Ken and Amos turned their attention to

the seven cars that made up the train. Four were freight cars, one was a baggage car, and two were passenger Pullmans.

They waited for a couple of minutes. It seemed that no one was going to get off at the Brookdale depot.

Then a man stepped down from the last car. He carried a suitcase in his right hand. A topcoat was draped over his left arm.

"That's him," Ken said.

The two boys ran back along the platform. Their flying heels made a hollow rumbling sound on the wooden planking. Then they were standing in front of the man, panting a little from the run.

"You—you're Lefty Gregory, aren't you?" Amos asked.

The man looked at them without answering. He was quite young. Yet, at the moment, Ken thought that he looked a little older than the twenty-three years the newspapers mentioned as his age. He was lanky—over six feet

The stranger carried a suitcase

tall—but there was a broadness to his shoulders that took away any appearance of thinness. His hands were long-fingered and firm. His hair was sandy, almost the color of Ken's, but his eyes were blue, while Ken's were greenish-brown. He was bareheaded and dressed in a neat bluish-gray suit.

"Yeah," he said finally, "I'm Lefty." Although he said it matter-of-factly, there was a tone of defense in his voice. It was as though he might be expecting trouble from admitting who he was. "Do I know you boys?"

"I'm Amos Jackson," the colored boy introduced himself quickly. "This is Ken Douglas. I just moved to Brookdale a few months ago. But Ken has lived here all of his life. He knew you when—when—"

"You mean he knew me *when,* period," Lefty said, forcing a smile. "Anyway, glad to meet you, Amos." Lefty put down the suitcase and stuck out his hand. Amos shook it eagerly.

"You didn't really quit the Cardinals, did

you?" Amos blurted out. "You—you just came home for a little rest, huh?"

It seemed to Ken that Lefty pretended not to hear the question.

"You say your name's Douglas?" Lefty asked, turning to him.

"Yep. Ken Douglas." He took the former major-league pitcher's firm hand in his own.

"Any relation to the Douglas who has the bakery over on Fourth Street?"

"He's my father," Ken said proudly.

"Makes the best chocolate éclairs in the country," Lefty said, smiling. "Say, you're a good fellow to know."

"You're not supposed to eat chocolate éclairs," Ken said. "Not when you're training for the big leagues."

"I can eat them now," Lefty said simply. "But, hey, how about telling me just why you fellows came down here to meet me? Or did you just happen to be here when the train pulled in?"

"No, we came to meet you," Amos assured him.

"Well, I appreciate it," the tall pitcher said. "Sure isn't like when I went away, is it? There were bands and pennants and everything. But, then, that's the way it goes, I guess. Besides, I don't blame anyone for not coming down. Didn't expect any parades."

"Oh, but no one knew you were coming, maybe," Ken said.

"You fellows knew," Lefty said. "Could have read it in the paper, couldn't they? Now, let's get to the real point. How come?"

Ken looked at Amos. Actually, he hadn't given it so very much thought. Amos had just seemed to think it was a good idea.

"We—we didn't want you to feel lonesome," the dark-skinned boy said. "It's no fun to feel lonesome."

"You're sure right," Left said thoughtfully. He reached out and rumpled Amos' short, curly black hair. "My folks would have come in from the farm to meet me, but I under-

28

stand my dad's car has gone haywire. Besides, I wasn't even sure which train I'd be on. So, fellows, thanks a lot. It helps to know I've got a couple good friends."

"Lefty," Ken said, as a new thought struck him, "we—we kind of thought you might teach us a few things. You know, the way they do it in the big leagues."

"You mean how they play baseball?" Lefty asked.

"Yeah."

"Sorry, kids," Lefty said, and his lips lost every trace of a smile. "No baseball. I'm through with baseball."

"But, Lefty," Amos said, "no one can be through with baseball. Not just like that." He snapped his fingers to emphasize the statement.

"I can," Lefty said firmly.

"Just because you—you beaned a player?" Amos asked.

Lefty seemed to flinch. "There's more to it than that," he said sharply.

"Would you tell us, maybe, sometime?" Ken asked.

"Look," Lefty said. "I appreciate you two coming down here to meet me, but I've got to catch a taxi home now. Come out and see me any time you feel like it. But not to talk baseball. Understand that? No baseball."

"We understand," Amos said.

"Yeah, we sure do," Ken said, scowling.

Lefty Gregory glanced at him as though not certain just how Ken had meant the remark. Then he turned and started toward the telephone booth.

"We might as well go," Amos suggested.

"Yeah," Ken said. "Let's. I'm not so sure that I like that guy."

"Why not?" Amos asked, surprised. "I think he's a pretty swell guy."

"Swell guy?" Ken scoffed. "How can anybody be a swell guy and quit his team just because he happened to bean ball a player? It still seems like a crazy thing to do."

Amos stopped and turned to face him.

"Well, if Lefty's crazy, then you're crazy, too," he said. "Why aren't you trying out for the Little League?"

"That's different," Ken insisted. "If you'd ever had your jaw broken by a wild pitch, I guess you'd. . . ."

"It's no different at all," Amos interrupted. "It's just a case of being on different ends of the accident, that's all. You're both afraid. Only in different ways."

"Who's afraid?"

"You are."

"Well, why aren't you playing, then?" Ken said hotly. "Just because your skin's a little different color, you're afraid the fellows won't want to play with you."

"I'm not afraid of being hit by an old ball," Amos shouted.

"Yeah, but you're afraid to play, anyway."

"I'll play!" Amos yelled. "I'll show you."

"I'll play, too," Ken yelled right back. "We'll see who shows who."

They stood glaring at each other. Then,

slowly, the anger began to leave their faces. Amos was the first one to break out with his easy friendly smile. Ken started to chuckle over the sudden outburst.

Then they began to laugh. When he was finally able to stop, Ken stuck out his hand.

"It's a deal?" he asked. "We'll play?"

"Let's go get your glove," Amos said.

They turned and started toward Ken's house.

CHAPTER THREE

They could hear the noise long before they reached the Brookdale Little League ball park. Then they were close enough to hear the solid crack of a seasoned ash bat on a horse-hide-covered baseball. The plop of other balls into fielders' gloves added to the mixture of sound.

It was all very pleasant to Ken's ears. Amos eagerly pounded a fist into the pocket of his own glove.

They went through a gate and stopped inside. The ball park was crowded with kids. They were all between the ages of eight and twelve. They were dressed in every fashion. Blue jeans, T shirts, and tennis shoes were by far the most common sight. Here and there a boy wore a baseball cap. A few had baseball shirts. There was even a small scattering of baseball pants, most of which had been Christmas presents.

But the Little League uniforms were not in sight. They wouldn't be handed out until later—not until spring practice was finished, and the actual team rosters were chosen.

There were a few men in the ball park. They were the managers and coaches of the league. They went among the boys, making a point here and dropping a playing hint there.

One of them spotted Ken and Amos. He walked over to them.

"Hello, boys," he said. "I'm Carl Foster. I'm secretary of our Little League. Have you boys signed up?"

"No, sir," Ken said. "We—we didn't decide to play until just this morning."

"Well," Mr. Foster replied, "the other boys have a week's jump on you. But it's still not too late to earn your place on one of the teams. The final choosing won't take place for a couple of weeks yet. Either one of you play last year?"

"No, sir," Amos said. "Ken had a broken jaw from playing sand-lot ball, and I didn't live here."

"Then I guess you're both rookies, huh?" Mr. Foster said quickly. He semed to note Amos' discomfort. "And you are both very welcome," he added. "How old are you?"

"I'm eleven," Ken said.

"Me, too," Amos answered.

"Good," the league secretary said. "You'll both have another year to play. You are eligible to play Little League ball as long as your thirteenth birthday doesn't arrive before August first. Come with me and we'll get a couple of registration cards. You will each have to take one home and get your mother's and father's signatures. I suppose it is all right with them if you play?"

Ken didn't figure that his parents would be so very keen for him to play. Not after last year's accident. Yet he didn't think that they would actually stop him. "I'm pretty sure I can play," he said, "as long as I keep up on my chores."

"That's often the case," Mr. Foster said, smiling.

"Hi, Ken," a boy yelled as he ran past chasing a ball.

"Hi, Corky," Ken called back. Actually, it was the first time they had spoken to each other since the big argument at Ken's house a week earlier.

"Hiyah, Ken," someone else called, but Ken couldn't tell to whom the voice belonged. He called "Hi," anyway.

Amos stood pounding the pocket of his glove. He kept smiling, but at nothing in particular.

Mr. Foster said, "There's an equal chance for everyone in Little League baseball. The best players make the teams. That's all there is to it. I hope you boys earn your positions." He was looking at Amos when he said it. "O.K., don't forget to bring those cards back tomorrow. Fill out every item, and have both parents sign on the lines there at the bottom. Now you can go and toss a few balls around if you want. I'll see you again."

Ken and Amos laid their cards on a bench in one of the players' dugouts in order not to get them bent and dirty.

Amos pulled a well-worn ball out of his hip pocket. They found a place along the third-base line and began throwing the ball back and forth, yet at every opportunity their gazes wandered to the different group of players. Ken knew a lot of them. There were many he didn't know. Some were older and some were younger than he and Amos. Some were pretty awkward. Some threw with stiff arm movements; their throws were neither swift

They began throwing the ball back and forth

nor accurate. Others were too loose or had little strength in their wrists. No doubt they would improve with practice, but some wouldn't improve enough to make a team.

Even though some probably knew this, they were still having fun.

Ken also noticed that there were plenty of good players on the field. Bruno, Corky, and Grant were almost a cinch to make a team. In fact, as last year's veterans of the Red Sox, they were practically certain to be Red Sox again this season. Corky had been voted the best outfielder in the league last year. He was a real ball hawk, and an above-average batter.

There were plenty of others, as good or better.

"We're sure going to have to work, aren't we, Ken?" Amos said, seeming to read Ken's thoughts.

"I'll say."

"We'll do it."

"Sure."

39

After a while the entire group was called together. They gathered in a large semicircle in front of the first-base dugout. One by one the men talked to them.

There were just two more weeks of spring practice, they pointed out. They warned that, although they hoped everyone would keep coming out, the boys must not let practice interfere with the next and last week of school.

They were glad to see eighty-three boys trying out for positions on the teams. They made it plain, however, that in two weeks the number would have to be cut to sixty. Fifteen players was the limit for the number of members on each team. Four teams would take sixty players. That meant twenty-three boys would not make it. But they should not be discouraged; they could try again the next year. Besides, they could keep playing in the minor league. Even though the minor-leaguers didn't get uniforms, they still would have plenty of fun playing with boys of their own baseball skills. They would be improving all of the time.

Dr. David Burton, President of the Brookdale Little League, was the last to speak. Although Dr. Burton was just about the busiest man in town, somehow he found time to devote to the boys. He looked a lot different now, Ken thought, than when the physician had set and doctored his broken jaw. Funny how different people seemed, depending upon where you met them and what they were doing.

"We're rolling now," Dr. Burton said, smiling, "and this looks like the finest group of boys in the country. Wouldn't doubt that we'll come up with a district-championship team. Maybe one team of you will even become section champs. That would put you in the regional play-offs. As you probably know, the eight regional winners of the United States play in the Little League world series in Williamsport, Pennsylvania, next August."

A wild cheer went up from the boys.

"Here we go!" Bruno Prosser yelled.

Dr. Burton smiled. "But, boys," he said, "don't count too heavily on any of the championships. Try, of course, but don't let it become the big thing. There are well over two thousand Little Leagues in the United States. Some are also in Alaska, Hawaii, Canada, the Panama Canal Zone, Cuba, and Puerto Rico —over eight thousand teams. That makes your chances about one in a thousand of ending up in Williamsport. On the other hand, there's no reason that one team can't be from Brookdale. The point is, play to win, but, above all, play to have fun. Baseball is as American as we are. We just go together, that's all. Let's keep it that way. Let's be real friends to the game. Even more important, let's be real friends to each other, even when the score is tied in the final inning and you are pitching to your neighbor on another team."

"I'll fan him!" Grant Emerson said, although not realizing that his words carried.

"That's right," Dr. Burton said with a

smile. "You fan him, if you can. But if he poles a home run out over the left-field fence to win the game, you take it like a good sport and still be friends. That's Little League; that's baseball; that's life—and that's the end of my speech."

Dr. Burton sat down on the bench, while the boys cheered themselves hoarse.

The sun was getting low on the western horizon when the players began to leave the ball park. Ken and Amos were going out between two sections of green-painted bleachers, when Bruno, Corky, and Grant caught up to them.

"Glad you decided to come out, Ken," Grant said. "You know, we've been practicing enough to tell. There aren't many good infielders in that bunch. Some, but not many. Why don't you try out for the keystone sack?"

"Second base?" Ken said. "But I've never played second."

"Never too young to try," Bruno said. He seemed to have forgotten all about their bitter argument a week ago.

"Amos is a better infielder than I am," Ken said.

"Could be," Corky said flatly. "But we could sure use you on second for the Red Sox. That is, if you are worth any credits when the players' auction comes up."

"Well, Amos and I will be out there trying," Ken assured the other boys.

Bruno said, "Good. Maybe there'll even be a place on one of the teams for Amos, too."

Ken didn't miss Bruno's meaning. He started to say something but thought better of it in front of Amos.

He glanced around. Silently, Amos had disappeared. Then he saw the colored boy cutting across a vacant lot by himself.

"Hey, Amos," Ken shouted, but his friend didn't turn to answer. "Wait for me, Amos. I go that way, too." He left Bruno, Corky, and Grant and started running to catch up with Amos.

But Amos was running too—running faster.

CHAPTER FOUR

Two weeks had gone by. Summer vacation was a week old when the long-awaited time for the players' auction arrived. A few of the original eighty-three boys had dropped out of practice. There were still around seventy-five at the ball park that day. The only adults on hand were a couple of the coaches. The team managers had gone to huddle with the player agent. He was the man who acted as auctioneer and moderator at the "sale."

Many of the boys knew just about where

45

they stood. They had played last season. Most of their positions were fairly secure for this year.

The new boys were the ones who were most tense on the field. They wondered for which team they would be chosen, if, indeed, they were chosen at all.

They wondered what their "credit value" was. But they would never know. That was a secret which only the player agent and the managers knew. And they wouldn't tell. It was not a good thing for one boy to know that he was rated as worth, perhaps, 2,000 purchase credits (which was like $2,000 in play money), while the fellow next to him was rated as worth only 500.

But all of the players knew that the bidding was an exciting event for the managers of the four teams. Soon each boy would know which team he was on, although he wouldn't know how much had been "paid" for his baseball talents.

The players' sale was handled just as they

are in the major leagues, only it was more secretive. In the Little League each manager had just so many credits. When the League was first formed he was given 36,000 credits with which to purchase players. Each year after that he was allowed an additional 10,000 credits. These he could add to any which he might have saved over from the previous season. It was just like putting money in the bank, except that the "money" was only good to buy players.

A manager had to spend his credits carefully. He might bid too high for a couple of pitchers, then find himself running out of credits with which to strengthen his infield.

Through careful purchasing, the good and not-quite-so-good players were equally divided among the four teams of the league. This system resulted in hard-fought games and close competition throughout the entire season.

It hadn't been an easy job to talk Amos back into coming out for practice after that first day. But the Negro boy had finally swallowed his hurt and had agreed to keep trying. First he had thought he would try for a place in the outfield, but Ken had coaxed him into third base.

"Let's stick together, Amos," he had said. "If we're lucky, we might even make the same team. You at third and me at second. You've got a good throwing arm. A third baseman has to have that for the long throw to first."

During the two weeks of practice there had been plenty of competition for the infield positions. Eight boys had wanted to be at second base. Seven wanted to land the third-base spots.

Ken didn't have any idea how he stood, but he figured that Amos had a good chance for third. He had never seen anyone try as hard as the colored boy did. And Amos was better than fair with the bat.

The batting practice had been Ken's big weakness. Now, as he picked a bat out of the rack and stepped up to the plate, he had that

48

same sinking feeling in the pit of his stomach. It had been there each time he tried to bat.

The pitch came toward the plate. Ken leaned back away from it.

"Strike one!" called one of the coaches, who was acting as practice umpire.

"Ken," another coach called, "guard that plate closer. You're too far back."

The farther back, Ken thought, the less chance of getting hit by a pitch. He heeded the instructions, however, and inched a little closer to the plate.

The next pitch whizzed toward him. It seemed to be coming in high and close. Ken jumped back quickly.

"Strike two!" the umpire called. "Right across the inside corner. Keep your eyes on those, son."

"It—it looked inside," Ken excused himself lamely. Yet he knew that he had stepped back before he even had made up his mind that the ball seemed to be inside.

"It wasn't," the umpire assured him.

He dropped the bat and walked away

Ken struck out on the next pitch. He dropped the bat and walked away dismally.

"You'll do better next time, Ken, boy," Amos encouraged, as he stepped up to the plate.

Ken didn't get another chance. Amos had just finished smacking a Texas leaguer out over second base, when the four team managers came into the park. They were all grinning. Thy knew how anxious the boys were to hear the results of the players' auction. Each manager carried a sheet of paper in his hand.

Practice stopped right then. The players rushed to crowd around the managers.

The manager of the Billings Hardware Giants was the first to read off his list of the fifteen boys who would make up the roster of the Giants' team. Each name was greeted with a quick cheer. After the fifteen names were read off, there were a few moans from players who had hoped to be on the Giants' list. After all, the Giants were also last year's league champs.

Next came the Rotary Club Tigers. The reactions were the same. Nor were they any different when the manager of the *Star-News* Pirates read off the names of his team.

By the time the third list had been read, there were forty-five happy players. After all, no matter which team each was on, the biggest joy was in being chosen at all.

The thirty players whose names hadn't been called stood around anxiously. Some twisted at the lacings on their gloves and mitts; others scuffed their shoes in the dirt; now and then, even a fingernail was bitten off. One thing was certain—not one of the thirty was at ease.

There was cause for wonder. They knew that the names of only half of them were on the list which Fire Captain John McGrath held in his hand. Fifteen of them would either drop down to the minor-league "farm" teams, or, if too discouraged, might give up.

Ken knew that there wouldn't be many giving up, though. They all liked baseball too much. Besides, a year of minor-league training would give them a much better chance to make the first team next season.

Ken glanced at Amos. As yet, neither of their names had been called. Both knew that they might not be called at all. There were quite a few good players among the thirty who waited.

Even worse, one of them might be called, but not the other. They had both counted so much on playing the season together. Even if they weren't on the same team, they could still practice together in their spare time. But now there was just one team left. They would both be Red Sox—or nothing.

Amos was holding onto his smile, but Ken could see it waver around the corners of his mouth.

"Don't worry," Ken whispered. Still, the palms of his own hands were moist with sweat.

"Well, fellows," Captain McGrath said, "seems that I'm in last spot. But you can be sure that this will be the only time the Red

Sox are in last place during the season."

There was a cheer from the thirty waiting boys. There was also a chorus of good-natured jeers from the boys already chosen for the other teams.

"Those of you whose names I don't call," Captain McGrath went on, "have no reason to feel bad. It doesn't mean that you can't play baseball just as well as some of the others. Perhaps some of you newcomers had a little bad luck during practice. Maybe you tried too hard. A year's seasoning on a 'farm' team will help to steady you down. Some of you will be the stars of next year's first teams. Remember, all Little Leagues are governed by a time-tested set of rules. One rule is that each team can have no less than twelve and no more than fifteen players on its final roster. We have a limited number of uniforms, catching gear, balls, bats, and other playing equipment. Please remember, if I do not call your name, it does not mean that you aren't a good player. Those whose names I do call showed up a little better during practice. Those, I'd like to see down at the firehouse this evening at six-thirty, if you can make it. Our team already has problems. I'll tell you about them later. Also, we'll pass out the uniforms this evening."

There was a cheer.

"O.K., here goes," Captain McGrath said.

Ken wasn't surprised to hear the names of Bruno, Corky, and Grant called out near the top of the list. They were veterans.

Beads of sweat were popping out on Ken's forehead. Then he heard Amos Jackson's name.

Amos' grin was big enough to hang one end on each ear. He held up his crossed fingers as a sign of good luck for Ken.

Ken hadn't been counting, but he knew that Captain McGrath was getting close to the bottom of the list.

". . . Ziggy Ross, Sam Silvers," the Red Sox manager continued reading. "And last, but not least, of course, Ken Douglas. Now, you boys who weren't chosen, please. . . ."

But Ken didn't hear any more of what Captain McGrath was saying. He spun around to face Amos.

"We made it, pal!" he shouted.

"Both of us," Amos said happily. "And on the same team. Wow!"

"Guess luck was on our side."

"Sure was."

Yet both of them knew that it was going to take a lot more than luck from then on. Neither one had missed noticing Bruno and Corky and Grant turn and walk away after the last name had been called.

CHAPTER FIVE

After dinner Ken helped his mother clear off the table.

"Is it all right if I go down to the firehouse now, Mom?" he asked.

"Of course, Kenneth," his mother said. "But it's a little early, isn't it? You said six-thirty."

"I want to stop by for Amos."

"Ken," his father called from the living room, "come here a minute, will you, please?"

Ken went in. His father was just laying down the evening *Star-News*.

"Son," his father said, "if I didn't sound very enthusiastic at the dinner table, about your making the team, that is, it was my error."

Ken had thought that his father had taken the good news somewhat matter-of-factly.

"I am proud that you made the team," his father went on. "But, of course, it wasn't so very easy for your mother and me to accept the fact that you were still going to play baseball. Not after last year's accident. But, of course, it would be foolish to stop drinking water just because the rains flooded your barn away once. Follow me, Ken?"

"I think so, Dad," Ken said.

"Besides, you're lucky there is such a good way to play as with the Little League," his father continued. "When I was a boy we didn't have a nice setup like that. It was strictly sand lot. No organization. No interested adults. Sometimes we were pretty selfish about who played on our teams. A lot of boys who should have been playing never got the chance."

"It's not that way in Little League, Dad," Ken said eagerly. "Everyone gets the same chance. It doesn't matter what his race, religion, or color is, either."

"That's the way it should be," his father said. "I see by the paper that Amos Jackson also made the Red Sox team."

"Amos plays good ball, Dad," Ken said.

"You and Amos have been chumming around quite a bit lately, haven't you?"

"I like Amos, Dad," Ken said quickly. "Amos is a swell kid. Maybe his family is kind of poor. Maybe there are more children than his father can keep dressed in new clothes and shoes, and plenty of food and—and—"

"They are always neat and clean," Mr. Douglas said, "and they are not getting into mischief. But what about the other fellows? I haven't seen Corky or Bruno or Grant around here for quite a while. You guys used to be pretty close friends. Anything happen?"

"I can't help it if they don't want to come over any more, Dad," Ken said. "They think I'm scared to play ball, because of my broken jaw last year."

"Is that all? You *are* playing ball."

"Well-l-l," Ken fumbled for the right words. "I think—that is, they think just because Amos is a—a—"

"A colored boy?" his father said quickly.

"I guess so," Ken said, then went on: "But, Dad, Amos is a swell guy. And if Bruno and those fellows get crazy ideas, well, that's up to them. The others don't feel any different toward Amos."

"And there's certainly no reason why they should," his father said. "You've decided to stick with Amos. Is that it?"

"I like Amos," Ken said stubbornly.

It was then that his father stepped over beside him. He put his arm around Ken's shoulders.

"Thanks, Son," he said. "I didn't want to

pry. But I kind of wondered just what was cooking between you fellows. Now, you better be getting down to the firehouse."

Ken started to turn away. He was a little puzzled.

"And, Son," his father said just before he reached the door, "there's just one other thing. I'm proud of you. Mighty proud."

Except for a couple of firemen who were playing ping-pong, the firehouse seemed vacant when Ken and Amos arrived.

"You fellows Little-Leaguers?" one of the firemen asked.

"Yes, sir," Amos said. "We're Red Sox."

"Good for you." The man smiled. "Then you better tear on upstairs before all of the uniforms are gone."

They didn't need a second prompting. Ordinarily they would have taken plenty of time to look over the bright-red pump engine, or the hook-and-ladder truck that was parked beside it. But not this evening. They swung past the shiny steel pole which the firemen used in sliding down from their upstairs sleeping quarters. They rushed up the narrow stairs two at a time.

"Hey, you two just made it," Captain Mc-Grath greeted them. "I began to think that maybe you had decided to go over to the Giants or something."

"We'd never do that," Ken said loyally.

"We're Red Sox," Amos added. "Through and through."

"That's the spirit," the fireman said, smiling. "And just for that I guess you rate a couple of uniforms." He led them over to a large table where the uniforms had been laid out.

"Wow!" Ken exclaimed. "They are real beauties."

"They get even better looking after you've made a few double put-outs and knocked in a half dozen runs or so," the team manager said. "I've seen them almost sprout wings after a home run. Let's see, Amos, you should take

62

about a size thirty-two uniform and a six-and-a-half cap. Here. Try 'em on for size."

"Oh, they'll fit," Amos said happily. He slipped the red-and-white shirt on over his T shirt.

"Ken, you're a little smaller," the team manager said. "Try this size thirty. With all that yellow hay on your head, you probably will need a larger cap."

"I'll be getting a butch haircut next week," Ken said.

"Well, if your cap slides down over your ears then, you can trade it in for a smaller size. We have a few extra caps. Here is a pair of baseball socks for each of you."

The socks were bright red with two broad white bands around the calf. There were no heels or toes in them. There was just a sort of belt that passed under the instep of the foot. But they were good heavy wool—fine protection against getting bruised or skinned during a slide.

"You wear your own short socks under

these," Captain McGrath said. "Regular white socks are best. But whatever you wear, just don't let me catch any of you fellows showing up at the ball park with those blinding fluorescent socks flashing on your feet."

He laughed, but Ken figured he meant it, anyway.

The uniforms fitted Ken and Amos perfectly.

"If any of your mothers object to laundering the uniforms," Captain McGrath announced, "bring them down here and we'll send them out with the fire-department laundry. Uniforms get dirty during a game. We expect that. But don't be showing up before a game in a dirty uniform. They belong to the league, and most of them can be used again next year. At the end of the season you may keep your caps. But the uniforms and other equipment have to be turned back in. O.K.?"

"O.K.," they chorused.

Then they eagerly went about checking over the other equipment. Bruno was particularly interested in the catcher's mitt with the Paul Richard signature on it. He tried on the mask and shin guards. The other players took turns standing off to one side of the room taking practice swings with different bats. When each found one that suited him best in length and weight, he read the name on it and would remember it for future use.

"Oh, fellows," Captain McGrath said, "I

forgot to mention one part of your playing equipment. Of course, everyone except the catcher has to furnish his own mitt or glove. It is up to everyone to have his own shoes. Tennis shoes are all right. If you can get the ones with the rubber cleats molded on the sole and heel, that's even better. They give you firmer footing and better traction in running. But remember, no metal cleats. Too dangerous for the Little League. Against the rules, too. O.K. Everybody got a uniform?"

"You bet," they answered.

"Then we're all set," the fireman said, "except for one final item. And it's a big one."

Some of the boys shot puzzled looks at each other.

"Find a place to sit down along the wall," the team manager instructed. "This is something that is going to take a bit of thought on the part of each of us. It's a pretty important problem if we are to hope for the league championship and a whack at the district and sectional play-offs."

67

Ken wondered if this was the problem that Captain McGrath had mentioned that afternoon at the ball park.

"No problem is too big for us," Bruno called. "Just let us get our teeth into it, Captain McGrath."

"We are a team without a coach," the fire captain announced.

"But we've got Mr. Boardman," Corky spoke up. "He has been out there every afternoon almost, and we thought. . . ."

"I thought so, too," Captain McGrath said. "So did Mr. Boardman. But I guess the insurance company for which he works didn't know about it. Mr. Boardman is being transferred to another territory."

"But he's a swell insurance man," Sam Silvers spoke up. "Why, my pop said. . . ."

Captain McGrath smiled. "Of course he's a good insurance man," he interrupted. "That's probably why his company is sending him out to open up a new territory. That's part of the business. The fact remains that

68

Mr. Boardman won't be able to act as your coach."

There was a groan.

"Now," the fire captain went on, "I'm not sure whether I'm doing this the right way or not, but it seems to me that the way to get a new and capable coach is to talk about it to the fellows he will be teaching. That's you."

The boys nodded. If they suggested a coach and he didn't turn out just right for them, it would be their own fault. A good coach was a great help to any team. A man who was willing to help, but who didn't know very much about baseball, was all right to a point.

An ideal Little League coach had to like kids. He had to be patient with them. And, very important, he had to know baseball and be able to teach it to the members of the team. Many Little-Leaguers were just beginners in the game. Faulty coaching, or the lack of real baseball know-how, could start poor playing habits that a fellow might have a hard time breaking later on.

". . . so," Captain McGrath was saying, "let's have your suggestions. But don't just come popping up with any name of some nice man you know. In addition to being a good guy, he has to be able to coach baseball. And coach it right."

Several mouths opened but clamped shut again. When they came right down to it, it was no simple task to think of a good coach. Almost every man was able to play base-ball, more or less, but few knew the game well enough to coach it.

"Of course," Captain McGrath said, "there are some men around town who would make suitable coaches. They are willing, also, most of them. But they find it impossible to arrange for the time it takes."

"How about Mr. Wright at the sporting-goods store?" Corky asked.

"He would be a good one, wouldn't he?" Captain McGrath agreed. "As a matter of fact, I called him. There's nothing he would like better. But his wife isn't well, and he has to run the store by himself. It is impossible for him to get away before six o'clock. But you can be sure he will be in the stands cheering whenever he can make it before the games are over. Who else can you think of?"

A silence came over the room.

"Come, come," Captain McGrath prompted, "there must be some other suggestions."

Still there was a thoughtful silence.

"Captain McGrath," Amos spoke up finally, "I think I know of someone who would be a swell coach. If we could get him to do it."

Ken glanced at Amos. He wondered who his friend could possibly have in mind.

"Who is it, Amos?" the Red Sox manager asked.

"Lefty Gregory."

It was almost like dropping a bomb in the middle of the group. A year ago the mention of Lefty's name would have been greeted by loud cheers from every boy in the room. But, as Ken well knew, feeling had changed greatly toward Lefty ever since he had quit the Cardinals.

71

The people of Brookdale, both young and old, had held great hopes for Lefty. They didn't understand his quitting the Cardinals. The reasons the newspapers gave didn't satisfy them. Maybe they didn't want to understand. Prides had been injured and tongues had wagged when Brookdale's prize big-league rookie had let them down—or so they thought.

"That's the nuttiest suggestion I ever heard." Bruno was the first to find his voice. "Amos, what's the matter with you, anyway?"

"There is nothing the matter with Amos," Ken defended his friend quickly. "Lefty would be a good coach. There is no one around here who knows as much about baseball as he does. No one who can play as good as he can, either."

"You mean when he played," someone said. "But now he's a has-been."

"How do you know?" first baseman Slats Eldred argued. "You don't really know why Lefty came home."

"He quit."

"Maybe he had good reason to."

Quickly the room was a noisy hodgepodge of private and group arguments over Lefty Gregory. It seemed to Ken that the opinion of the fellows were pretty evenly divided for or against Lefty.

It was Captain McGrath who finally quieted the room with a loud "Hold it!"

The rumble of excited voices quickly died down.

"That's about as fine a display of poor team spirit as I have ever had the misfortune to witness," the fire captain scolded. "If this is a sample of the way it's going to go, maybe all of you better turn in your uniforms right now, and save your mothers the job of laundering them. It's a cinch you'll never win any ball games in them if this is a sample of what's in store for the Red Sox."

Every one of the fellows hung his head sheepishly. It was nearly a minute before any of them got enough courage to look up. During all of that time Captain McGrath just

73

stood there in front of them, silently looking from one player to another.

"All right," he said finally. There was no longer any anger in his voice. "Where were we? Oh, yes. Amos had just made the suggestion that we try to get Lefty Gregory to be our coach. Now, let's try it the right way. One at a time, will you fellows get up and make your objections?"

Not one of the players moved.

"Bruno," Captain McGrath said, "you didn't have any trouble finding plenty of words a couple of minutes ago. You want to carry on?"

Bruno swallowed hard. "No, sir," he said, "and—and I'm sorry that I popped off. But, anyway, I don't think Lefty would agree to coach us, even if he was asked."

"I don't think so, either," shortstop Brick Osborn said.

"Well," Captain McGrath said, "he won't even be asked unless I'm sure it is all right with every member of this team, and also un-

74

less I am sure that every player will be fair with him and follow his instructions if he should accept. I'm not saying how I feel about it. It's your team, and you should have some say in how it operates. Now, do you want to ask Lefty, or don't you?"

Several heads nodded.

"Let's ask him," Sam Silvers said.

"We've got to have a coach," Ziggy Ross added.

"Who doesn't want him to be asked?" Captain McGrath said. "Raise your hands."

There was no sound—no raising of hands.

"Well, that leaves just one more thing," the Red Sox manager said. "Lefty hasn't been seen in town but once or twice since he came home several weeks ago. He doesn't seem to want to meet people. Just stays out on the family farm. Now, I would be willing to run out there and ask Lefty. I doubt if that would be the best way, however."

"I'll go out and see him, Captain McGrath," Amos spoke up. "We—Ken and me—met Lefty

75

at the depot when he got home. We know him. He's a real good guy."

"I'll go with Amos," Ken volunteered quickly.

"That sounds like a good idea," Captain McGrath said. "I think you two may do a better job of convincing Lefty that the Red Sox need him than I could. But if it's true that Lefty has sworn off baseball, you may not find it easy. In any case, bring back his decision by Monday. Our first league game is scheduled for Thursday afternoon. We'll have to get a coach before then—the sooner the better."

Ken had a feeling that Captain McGrath was right when he said that it might not be easy to get Left Gregory to coach the Red Sox, but neither he nor Amos had any idea how really tough it was going to be.

CHAPTER SIX

The Gregory farm was nearly a mile north of town. Amos didn't own a bicycle, so he and Ken decided to walk. The distance seemed short as they ambled along, trying to figure just what was the best way to ask Lefty Gregory to be the Red Sox coach.

"He can't do any more than tell us 'no,' " Ken said.

"That's what we've got to keep him from doing." Amos kicked a stone out of the rutted dirt road. "And, remember, that day at the depot he did invite us to come out and visit him."

"Yeah," Ken said, "but he also warned us not to come out to talk baseball. Remember that?"

"I'm trying not to," Amos said, smiling. "Hey, there's the place now," he pointed. "Over there under those elms and cotton-woods."

"Well, cross your fingers," Ken said, as they turned in the open gateway.

The farmhouse was a neat two-story frame building—not big, but not small. It was painted a clean white. The doors and windows were trimmed in green. Slightly behind and to one side was a small screened-in structure about the size of Ken's bedroom at home. He guessed it was the summer kitchen. Probably it was also the laundry room. Through the screen, he caught a glimpse of a cream separator.

Across the farmyard was a large red barn. Beyond it were several small sheds. A concrete silo speared skyward at the far end of the barn.

In the fenced fields the black and white of a dozen or so Holstein cows stood out against the green pasture grass. Chickens scurried around the barnyard. From the direction of the small sheds came the noisy oink-oink of pigs.

"Boy, oh, boy!" Ken said. "This is some farm, huh?"

"Really is," Amos said enviously. "Even all my brothers and sisters would have room to run around out here. Hey, watch out. Here comes a big dog."

He was big, all right—big and white and spotted with brown. He came bounding around the house toward them.

"Let's get out of here," Amos said quickly.

"Look at his tail," Ken said. "Waggin' like crazy. Hi, fella." He whistled softly. It was as much a gesture to keep up his own courage as a sign of friendship to the dog.

The dog stopped just short of them. He began to bark, but his tail kept wagging.

The back door of the farmhouse opened.

Lefty Gregory came out onto the stoop. He was dressed in blue overalls and a lighter blue shirt, and he carried a straw hat in his hand.

"Hi—hi, Lefty," Ken said.

"Well, if it isn't my two friends from the depot," Lefty said, smiling. "Down, Prince. He's O.K., boys. He won't bite you."

"Better tell *him*, Lefty," Amos said. "Maybe he doesn't know it."

But the dog stopped barking. He went up to the boys and let them pet him.

"Let's see," Lefty said, putting on his hat and walking out to them. "You're Amos, aren't you?"

"That's me."

"And you're Douglas — Ken Douglas. Right?"

"Right," Ken said. "You told us at the depot that we could come out to see you. Remember?"

"Sure, I remember," Lefty said, "and I'm glad you took me up on it. But. . . ." He looked at the fielders gloves which both Amos and Ken carried strapped around the belt loops of their trousers.

"Oh," Ken said quickly, "we didn't come out to play ball. Amos and I always have our baseball gloves with us. We're Little-Leaguers."

"I see," the tall left-hander said, smiling. "And I guess you never know when you might just stumble upon a game. Well, O.K., but don't. . . ."

Ken had not figured on bringing up the subject just yet, but he didn't want Lefty to have a chance to say "no" even before the question was asked.

"Were you ever a baseball coach, Lefty," he asked quickly.

"Me? No," Lefty said. "Soon as I graduated from State College I started playing baseball on minor-league farm teams. Then I got boosted out to the West Coast." Lefty's blue eyes had a faraway look in them. "I played a while with Los Angeles. Then, this year. . . ." Suddenly he stopped, and his eyes focused back on Ken. "But, see here, we weren't going to talk baseball."

"I—I guess we just can't help but talk baseball," Amos said. "We're Red Sox."

"They don't show," Lefty said, smiling.

"The Red Sox is the fire-department team," Ken explained. "We just got our uniforms yesterday. Boy, they are really swell. Red and white, with real baseball stockings, too. These are the caps. We can wear them all we want. But we are only allowed to wear our uniforms at games."

"But it doesn't look like the Red Sox are going to have a very good chance in the league," Amos said. "We haven't got a coach."

Lefty's eyes widened. "Oh, so that's it," he said. "I don't suppose there is any chance of that being the reason you came out to see me. You wouldn't be after me to be your coach? Now, look here, you two—"

"Please, Lefty," Ken cut in. "All of the fellows agreed —er, want you. And Amos and I promised—well, almost promised. We said we'd ask. . . ."

The scowl slipped slowly off of Lefty's face. "Fellows," he said, "I appreciate your thinking of me. And I think that Little League baseball is swell, too. But I told you before that I just want to forget baseball. Can't you understand that?"

"No," Amos said, "I can't understand anyone wanting to forget baseball."

"Just because you beaned a player is no real reason to quit baseball, is it, Lefty?" Ken asked.

The tall pitcher was silent for a moment. He looked sharply at Ken. For a second Ken thought he was going to be angry. Then Lefty let out his breath in a sort of long sigh.

"There is more to it than that," he said. Then he shrugged. "Well, I guess you fellows won't be satisfied until you know the whole story. Come on, sit down."

The three of them sat on the cement curbing that formed a circle around the water cistern.

"As you may know," Lefty began, "I went up pretty fast in baseball. Three years out of college and I was in the majors. Oh, a lot of other guys have gone up fast, too. Fellows like Ralph Kiner, Jackie Robinson, Paul Pettit, Micky Mantle. I could probably name a dozen more."

"Bobby Feller?" Ken asked.

"Yeah, Bobby was a real boy wonder," Lefty said. "But that was quite a few years ago."

"He's still a good pitcher," Amos said.

"He sure is," Lefty agreed. "I only wish I was half as good."

"You're more than that," Amos said. "Just because you threw one bean ball doesn't make you a bum pitcher."

"I wish it were only *one* bean ball," Lefty said thoughtfully. "But bean balls have been my weak spot ever since I started pitching baseball."

"We didn't know that," Ken said.

"Oh, I never really hurt a player with one before," Lefty said. "And goodness knows I tried hard enough to break myself of the fault. But when I'm trying to hook a high curve to a right-handed batter—well, I just can't seem to get the right break to the ball. Either there's too little, for a called ball, or there's too much curve. If there's too much, it becomes a bean ball."

"Jeepers," Ken said, "that seems an easy enough problem to solve. Just don't throw high curves to right-handed batters. Feed him a fast ball, or a knuckler, or something else."

Lefty smiled. "You might be able to get by with it in some of the minor leagues," he said, "but a big-league pitcher has got to be able to use every pitch, or he's just not a major-league pitcher, that's all. I—I'm just not good enough for the majors."

"Lefty," Amos said, "if that's true why didn't you just go back to the minors? Maybe the American Association, or back to the Pacific Coast League. You could work yourself back up again, couldn't you?"

"There is just one reason, Amos," Lefty said. "I lost my heart for baseball after I put Johnny Logan in the hospital."

Ken saw the sweat break out on the south-paw pitcher's forehead.

"But Mr. Logan's all right now, isn't he?" Amos asked.

"I'm afraid not," Lefty said. "He's out of the hospital. He's home, but he is still in bed. The doctors don't know yet how bad his head injury is."

"We wear head-protector helmets when we bat in the Little League," Amos said. "Have to."

"A few fellows in the big leagues wear them, too," Lefty said. "Johnny Logan didn't."

"Johnny Logan isn't mad at you, is he?" Ken asked.

"Johnny's still my friend," Lefty said simply. "I don't know if you fellows will understand what I'm trying to say, but—well, the fun I always have had out of playing baseball left me the moment I saw Johnny lying on the ground with his head bleeding."

Ken couldn't help but shudder. He was remembering how he had been knocked to the ground, also. He was remembering the blood on his own face, and the taste of it in his mouth.

"Whillikers," Amos said, "people get hurt all of the time. You can't help that. A lot of them slip in bathtubs, even."

"Of course," Lefty agreed. "But—well, baseball was always a game to me."

"It is to all of us," Ken said. Yet he remembered that all during the time his broken jaw was healing he had felt much the same way as Lefty did. He wasn't too sure that he didn't feel somewhat the same way now.

"It just doesn't seem like a game any more," Lefty said firmly. "Not to me. I don't like to feel that way, but there it is."

Ken and Amos looked at each other. Neither one could think of anything to say.

"I—I guess I know how you feel, Lefty," Ken said finally. Then, almost without realizing it, he was blurting out the story of his own injury, and how he practically had decided not to play any more.

"Well, I'm glad you decided to play, after all," Lefty said after Ken had finished. "Baseball's a really swell game for kids."

"I think it's a good game for everyone," Amos said. "Doesn't matter how old he is."

Ken was doing some fast thinking. "I don't know," he said. "After hearing Lefty, I've got a good mind to turn back my uniform. There are a lot of other games where a fellow doesn't have to take a chance of getting beaned—or of beaning someone. Isn't that right, Lefty?"

"Hey," the southpaw pitcher said quickly, "you've got me all wrong. Don't you quit baseball. The chance of getting hurt playing baseball is one in a million. Maybe even less."

"But you hurt someone and you quit," Ken insisted. "I got hurt. I don't like to get hurt any more than anyone else does. Maybe I better quit, too."

"It's different with me," Lefty said.

"How?"

"It just doesn't seem possible that anyone would want to forget baseball," Amos said.

Lefty looked from one to the other. "Seems to me," he said, "that you two are trying to lead me into some kind of a trap. I wish I could change my feelings toward playing baseball. I really wish I could. I've tried hard enough. But I just haven't got what it takes any more. It's just not there. I'm sorry."

"We're sorry, too," Ken said. "Yeah, I guess we were kind of trying to lead you into a trap, Lefty. Maybe we hoped that you would change your mind. But I guess kids shouldn't try to outthink grownups, huh?"

Lefty smiled. "Thanks for trying, anyway."

"Sure, Lefty," Amos said. "But, anyway, I guess we had no right to snoop."

"I don't mind," Lefty said. "Guess it did me good to get it off my chest."

"We really didn't come out here to snoop, Lefty," Ken said. "We came out here to ask if you wouldn't coach the Red Sox. But I guess a guy couldn't coach and forget baseball at the same time, could he?"

"Not very well," the left-hander said

89

thoughtfully. "But, then, it wouldn't be exactly like playing, either, would it?"

"No," Amos said quickly. "And a coach could teach us how to play so that we wouldn't get hurt, or wouldn't hurt anyone else."

Lefty tugged at his chin. "You might have something there, at that," he said.

"We sure wish you would coach us," Ken said.

"We sure do," Amos confirmed.

"The fellows will scalp us if we don't get you to be our coach." Ken could see that Lefty was weakening a little.

"We told them you were a real guy," Amos added.

"Whoa, now." Lefty held up a hand. "You two are fanning me out."

"We're not pitching curves."

"They're straight balls, Lefty," Amos said. "We need you."

Ken thought he saw an almost eager look creep into the former big-league pitcher's blue eyes. It certainly wasn't the look of a fellow who really truly wanted to forget about base-ball.

"When is the next Red Sox practice?" Lefty asked.

"This afternoon," Ken said. "In just a couple of hours."

"Where's the ball park? There wasn't any Little League park when I lived here, you know."

"We'll show you where it is," Amos said eagerly.

"O.K., fellows," Lefty said. "You win. I'll have a try at it. How about waiting until I climb out of my overalls?"

"We'll wait," they yelped happily. "And how, we'll wait!"

CHAPTER SEVEN

The *Star-News* Pirates had just left the diamond after their pregame warm up. The Fire Department Red Sox were grouped around Lefty Gregory in front of the home-team dugout. The green-painted bleachers were filled with young people and adults. Some of the players' mothers were going along the aisles selling peanuts, popcorn, and soda pop. Any money that was made would go toward helping future Little League teams.

People were laughing and joking, but there was an air of tension over it all. Brookdale took its Little League baseball seriously.

It was Thursday afternoon. The first game of the regular season was just about to get under way.

"Now, look, fellows," Lefty said, as his eyes swept over the fifteen grim faces gathered around him. "Loosen up. Relax. You can't play good ball if you've got yourselves tied up in knots. Except you, Brick." Lefty smiled and pointed to Brick Osborn's feet. "You could stand a little tying up on that shoestring."

Blushing over his carelessness, Brick dropped to one knee and wound the loose shoelace into a firm double bow.

"This is our first game, as you know," Lefty went on. "Nobody's going to expect you to play perfect baseball, either in the field or at bat. So if you bobble one, or strike out, just forget it and try harder next time. If you will do some of the things I've tried to coach you in during the past two weeks, it might help. It won't cure everything, but it might help."

Ken knew it would help him. The other fellows were nodding. Those two weeks of practice had been long, tiring ones. Lefty was quite a taskmaster. Yet, he had never lost patience or bawled out any of the players for making errors. All he asked was that they try their best.

He hadn't even bawled out Ziggy Ross when the speedy left fielder kept running in and mis-judging fly balls that went sailing over his head toward the fence.

Time and again Lefty told Ziggy to pause for a count of one after the ball left the hitter's bat. That split-second pause would give Ziggy a chance to judge how hard the ball was hit and just where it was going. Knowing this, when Ziggy made his first move, it would be in the right direction.

But Ziggy had kept moving the instant he heard the crack of the bat on the ball. Then he would try to change his direction. Half of the time he wouldn't get to the ball. Finally, how-ever, Ziggy had forced himself to follow Lefty's advice.

Since he had gotten onto the one-count method for sizing up the hit, Ziggy had missed only one fly ball during practice. He didn't figure to miss any today.

Lefty had quickly proved himself a good coach of any position, not just pitching alone. It wasn't surprising, though. Lefty had played both infield and outfield positions in high school and early college. That was before he had turned to pitching.

Lefty even knew how to play the catcher's position. Bruno had always squatted in a square-away stance behind the plate. Lefty had shown the catcher how to squat with his right foot a few inches back. Then, as soon as Bruno straightened up after a catch, he was in ready position to throw. The husky catcher was a little doubtful at first, but as soon as he got onto it, his pegs to second base were faster and surer.

From that time on, Bruno was strictly on Lefty's side.

The former big-leaguer had given every Red Sox player some valuable pointers.

After the first couple of days there had been

no further talk about whether Lefty's quitting the Cardinals had been right or wrong.

Yet, so far, Lefty had been unable to correct one fault on the Red Sox team. No matter how much Lefty had tried to talk him out of it, Ken just couldn't break himself of the habit of ducking back away from the plate every time a pitch came toward him which looked even a little bit close.

"I'm trying, Lefty," Ken had said one day. "I just can't help it." He had been near to tears. But he blinked them back quickly so the coach wouldn't get any idea that he was chicken.

"Well, Ken," Lefty had said with a slight shrug of resignation, "I can't hog-tie you to the plate. But something has to be done. It isn't— Well, an infielder who can't get in his swats at the plate won't help us win many ball games."

Ken hadn't missed the real meaning behind Lefty's words. The big southpaw pitcher played no favorites. Lefty would take him out of the line-up just as quickly as he would any-one else, even though, Ken thought, he and Amos were a little closer friends to the left-hander than were the rest of the boys.

And here was the first game, about to start, and Ken hadn't been able to break himself of his fear at the plate.

"O.K., fellows," Lefty said. "Here is the starting line-up. You will bat in the order in which I call your names. You can check it on the scorebook when you come in to bat in the last half of the first inning."

The players listened eagerly as Lefty read off the names. Ken wasn't at all sure he would be playing second base. After all, there were Bobby Lubbock and Peewee Baker and a couple of other fellows who might be picked. Besides, Lefty didn't believe that Little-Leaguers should specialize too much; he thought they should be able to play wherever they were needed. This didn't hold true for the pitchers. They had to watch their arms more closely. But Lefty didn't believe that even pitchers should specialize, until after they had played other positions and were certain that pitching was what they wanted to do— and what they could do best.

The Red Sox coach read off the line-up:

Brick Osborn—ss (shortstop)
Ziggy Ross—lf (left field)
Amos Jackson—3b (third base)
Corky Richards—rf (right field)
Sam Silvers—cf (center field)
Bruno Prosser—c (catcher)
Slats Eldred—1b (first base)
Ken Douglas—2b (second base)
Grant Emerson—p (pitcher)

"All right, fellows, that's the starting line-up," Lefty said. "Get out there, now. And let's have plenty of the ol' hubba-hubba. Talk it up all the time. Give Grant plenty of support. Good luck."

The team formed a circle and stacked their hands over each others' in a quick shake. Then, with a loud whoop, they raced out to their positions on the diamond.

A roaring cheer went up from the crowd.

Ken scooped a practice grounder that Slats threw his way, straightened up, and whipped it to first.

"That's the ol' wing," Slats called.

It helped to erase the thought which had been preying on Ken's mind—the thought of being next to the last in the batting order. Oh, it wasn't that there was anything really wrong with being way down on the batting line-up, but to Ken it indicated that the coach figured he was weak in the hitting department.

Ken also knew that if he hoped to hold down second base during the season, he was going to have to prove up as a batter.

"Play ball!" the plate umpire called.

The lead-off batter for the Pirates stepped up to the plate, and the game was under way.

On the two-ball, one-strike pitch, the batter smacked a looping fly out over second base. Ken started running back. Then he caught sight of Sam Silvers tearing in toward the ball. He heard Sam's yell. He peeled off in order not to collide with the center fielder. Sam made a nice running catch for the first out.

Grant fanned the next batter. The third Pirate made a clean hit over Amos' head into short left field. But he was left stranded on first, when the cleanup batter smacked a line drive which Slats jumped up and speared in his trapper first baseman's mitt.

The Red Sox raced in for their turn at bat.

Their luck at the plate was no better than the Pirates' had been. Three up and three down—two fly balls and a close play from third to first that put Amos out by half a step.

The first inning was a good sample of things to come. It was a close scoreless ball game through the first three full innings.

Then, in the top half of the fourth, the first Pirate batter hit a blooper into right field for a single. The next laid down a sacrifice bunt, moving the runner to second.

A pop fly to Ken made it two away.

Then the roof fell in. The Pirate catcher, their strongest batter, got hold of one of Grant's fast pitches. Out in left field Ziggy Ross paused just long enough to count his "one." Then he turned and started chasing after the soaring ball.

But it kept right on soaring. It soared over the left-field fence for a home run.

Pirates 2, Red Sox 0.

Grant fanned the next batter, but the real damage already had been done.

"Don't worry about it," Lefty Gregory said, as the grim-faced team trotted in to bat in their half of the fourth inning. "Just start hitting that apple and get back those runs. Brick, you're up. Keep that bat off your shoulder. When you swing, swing straight through. You are striding into the pitch too much. Shorten it up. Take about a six-inch stride. Just enough to put yourself into a natural position to hit the ball. Easy does it. Let's go."

Brick followed Lefty's instructions and smacked the second pitch into deep left field for a double. Ziggy Ross flied out. Then Amos got hold of a low curve and dropped a Texas-league single between shortstop and center field. Brick scored.

Pirates 2, Red Sox 1.

Ken felt the ball smack into his glove

That ended the scoring for the inning. Nor was either team able to squeeze a run in during the fifth, although the Red Sox did get two runners on base.

The sixth and final inning began, with the Pirates still leading by one run.

Out on the pitcher's mound, Grant bore down for all he was worth. He was tense and seemed to be trying too hard. He walked the first man up. The next batter attempted a sacrifice bunt. But, wisely, Grant kept the pitches high. The bunt popped up into the air. Amos scurried in and took it on the fly.

Desperate to get into scoring position, the runner dug out for second after Grant's next pitch. But Ken had expected it. He was covering the bag when Bruno's throw came in low and fast. Ken felt the ball smack into his glove just before he dipped it down to tag the runner's sliding foot.

"Your-rr-r *out!*" The base umpire jerked his thumb up over his right shoulder.

That ended the threat. The next Pirate

batter dribbled an easy grounder down the first-base line. Slats took it and touched the bag for an unassisted put-out to retire the side.

"It's now or never, Corky," Slats said, as the small right fielder went to the bat rack. "Just get a bingle, pal. We'll bring you in."

And Corky got a bingle, just out of the third baseman's reach. Corky pulled up on first, grinning. He represented the tying run, if they could just work him around.

Slats, a left-hander, took his signal from the coach at third. Everyone on both teams knew pretty well that it would be a sacrifice bunt. The Pirate third baseman played in close on the infield grass. The first baseman stood ready to charge in.

Slats let the first pitch go by for a ball. He bunted the second pitch squarely down the first-base line. The first baseman grabbed it, but it was too late to make a play for second. He tagged Slats as he raced past.

But the sacrifice bunt had worked. The tying run was now on second.

Sam Silvers strode to the plate. He smacked

a two-and-two pitch for a hot grounder toward shortstop. The Pirate infielder booted the ball. Corky sprinted to third. Sam reached first on the error. One away.

The crowd was going wild.

The Pirates were rattled by the error. The first pitch to Bruno went into the dirt. The Pirate catcher scrambled for it, while Sam streaked to second. There was no chance for Corky to steal home with the tying run. The ball had not slipped far enough past the catcher.

Bruno hit under the second pitch, lobbing a high fly ball just over the pitcher's head. Bruno slammed his bat into the dirt, as the Pirate second baseman smothered the ball for the second out.

"Lay off that bad-temper stuff, Bruno," Lefty Gregory scolded mildly from the dugout.

Now it was up to Ken. A hit would easily bring in the tying run, and probably the winning one, also.

106

Ken dropped one of the two bats he had been using for his practice swings. He adjusted the plastic head-protecting batter's helmet over his ears and stepped to the plate. He heard the shouts of his teammates, and the cheers of the rooters in the stands. He also heard some razzing from Pirate fans. But he didn't pay any attention. Only one thing really mattered: He had to get a hit.

He glanced toward the first-base coach, just in case there was any kind of a sign on. Yet he knew there wouldn't be. He was on his own, to hit or take as he saw fit.

The first pitch came in fast and inside. He jumped back quickly.

"Strike one!" the umpire called.

"Strike one?" Ken stepped out of the batter's box and turned to the umpire. "It was way inside, ump."

"You just keep your eyes on the ball, son," the umpire said. "I'll do the figuring whether they're over the plate or not."

Determined not to step away from the next

pitch, Ken crowded the plate. The pitch was low and outside for a ball. Then another ball. Ken fouled the next pitch into the stands for a two-and-two count.

"Now pickle one, Ken, ol' boy," Amos called from the dugout. "You can do it."

"I'll do it, Ken thought to himself as he bent down to rub dirt on his sweaty hands.

The Pirate pitcher took his windup. The ball came sizzling in. It looked close—too close. It seemed to be shooting toward his head.

In a frantic effort, Ken tried to back away. But just as he did, the ball started to hook in toward the plate. He had backed away too soon.

He knew he was afraid.

"Strike three!" the umpire bellowed, jerking off his mask and walking away.

The ball game was over.

Pirates 2, Red Sox 1.

Without glancing toward his teammates or Lefty Gregory or anybody, Ken dropped the bat and started running. He vaulted the low side-line fence and kept on. He didn't stop until he had reached his home, hurried into his room, and flopped face down on his bed.

It was then that his feet stopped running, but the tears started.

CHAPTER EIGHT

Ken's breakfast cereal didn't seem to have much taste to it the following morning. He wasn't even interested in the pictures on the cereal carton. The offer of a "Jet Helicopter" for ONLY 25 cents and a box top went unnoticed.

"What's the matter, Kenneth?" his mother asked. "You have hardly touched your breakfast."

"The Red Sox had a little bad luck yesterday," Ken's father explained. "Sorry that I couldn't make the game, Ken. But, then, perhaps it is just as well." He paused, then said,

"I wouldn't have enjoyed seeing you run away."

So, Ken thought dismally, his father had heard.

"I—I couldn't help it, Dad," Ken explained lamely.

"Yes, I believe you could have, Son," Mr. Douglas said. Yet, there was no unkindliness in his voice or in the way he looked at Ken. "You know, your mother and I weren't so very anxious to sign that card to let you play Little League baseball."

"We certainly weren't," Ken's mother said, turning from the stove. "That broken jaw last year was no fun for any of us. We didn't want to have to go through anything like that again. Or to have you go through it."

"But," his father went on, "if a person gets stung by a bee it is no reason that he should avoid clover patches the rest of his life. Know what I mean, Ken?"

"Yes," Ken said.

"I might as well tell you," Mr. Douglas continued, "I talked to Captain McGrath last night. McGrath tells me that you're afr— that is, shy at the plate. You keep backing up. I can understand it some, Ken. You keep remembering your accident. Right?"

"I—I guess so, Dad."

"Yet, that accident was just one of those things. Probably wouldn't happen again in fifty years. Don't you know that's true? You even have plastic helmets to protect you when you're at bat in a Little League game. You didn't have that in sand-lot ball. As I recall, you even told me after the accident that you weren't keeping your eye on the ball. Remember?"

"Yes."

"Well, Ken," his father went on, "backing up can get to be a pretty bad habit. Running away is even worse. There ought to be another way, Son—a better way."

"I've tried, Dad," Ken blurted out. "I've really tried. But I—I can't seem to whip it."

"There's no problem in the world that can't

be whipped," Mr. Douglas said firmly. "And 'can't' is a poor attitude to have on your team. Can you think of anybody who has had a problem that he hasn't found some answer for—if he really tried?"

"Lefty," Ken said, almost without realizing it.

"Lefty Gregory?"

"Yes."

His father was silent a moment. "Maybe Lefty hasn't tried as hard as he should," he said finally.

"Oh, but he has, Dad," Ken insisted. "He really has."

"I wonder," his father said simply. "Anyway, it is too bad that he hasn't found the right answer. I was reading on the sports page last night that the Cardinal manager is trying to get Lefty to report back to the team. Seems that the Cards are in bad need of some good pitching."

"Golly," Ken said, "I sure wish Lefty would pitch. He's a swell fellow, Dad."

"But the Cards' manager also mentioned

that he didn't want Lefty to return to the team unless Lefty himself really wanted to. A half-hearted ballplayer is worse than no player at all."

"I'm afraid Lefty won't go back," Ken said, remembering the day he and Amos had talked to the big southpaw pitcher.

"Well, I've got to get off to work," his father said. He folded his napkin and pushed back from the table. "And let's not have any more running away from anything. O.K., Ken?"

"I won't, Dad," Ken promised. "I won't."

"Good boy." His father patted Ken's shoulder and left.

Ken had just finished helping with the breakfast dishes, when he heard Amos call from outside.

"I got up early and did all my work," Amos said proudly. "What are you figuring on doing today, Ken?"

Ken had made up his mind as soon as he was awake that morning. "I think I'll go out to see Lefty," he said.

"Special reason?" Amos asked.

"I want to tell him that I'm sorry I ran away after the game yesterday," Ken said. "I—I guess it was a pretty bum thing to do."

Amos was silent. Ken was glad that Amos didn't start blaming him. He felt he had had just about all the blame he could stand that morning.

"How about me going along?" Amos asked. "Maybe we can kind of play catch on the way out. Have to keep in practice for our game with the Tigers Thursday. I've got a mitt and a ball."

He didn't need to say that. The mitt was as big as life, hanging as usual from the belt loop. The ball fairly strained the seams of his hip pocket.

"Besides," Amos added as a clincher, "I want to ask Lefty about how to play a grounder to my right. I was off balance on a couple of throws yesterday."

"You didn't make any errors," Ken said.

"Guess I was lucky."

Ken asked his mother if it was all right to

go out to Lefty's. After promising to be back in time for lunch and lawn mowing, he and Amos started out.

Lefty's mother answered their knock on the back door of the farmhouse. "I think you will find him out in the barn," she said, smiling.

Lefty was repairing a latch on one of the milking stanchions.

"Hi, fellows," he greeted. "Don't tell me there's a ball game going on out this way."

"Lefty," Ken said quickly. He wanted to get it off his chest before he lost courage. "I—I want to tell you I'm sorry that I ran away yesterday after—after I lost the game."

"You didn't lose the game," Lefty said. "Get that idea out of your head. We lost the game. The team. Anyone else might have fanned out just as easily as you. But—well, you shouldn't have run away."

"I know."

"Well, as long as you know, and as long as you won't do it again, I guess that takes care of it. It was swell of you to come all the way out here to tell me you were sorry. You didn't need to."

"I wanted to," Ken said.

"Amos," Lefty said, "hold this chain together for me, will you? I've got to squeeze that link closed. One of the cows got her head out of the stanchion and practically walked away with the milking machine this morning."

"Maybe she wanted to deliver the milk to the creamery herself," Amos said, laughing.

They all laughed. Ken felt good that Lefty had taken his apology so easily. Lefty really was swell.

They had left the barn, when the tall pitcher brought up the subject which Ken knew was long past due.

"You had a little trouble standing up to the plate yesterday, didn't you, Ken?" he asked.

"I—I guess so," Ken admitted.

"Same old trouble?"

"I tried, Lefty," Ken insisted. "I really tried."

"But it wasn't quite enough, huh?"

"I guess not."

"Well, you're going to have to work on it harder," Lefty said. "I'm afraid you won't be able to hold down a regular spot on the Red Sox unless you break yourself of being plate shy. In the first place, you are off-balance from the moment you step up to bat."

"How do you mean?" Ken asked.

"You stand with your foot in the bucket."

"What's that?"

"He means you keep your left foot back," Amos explained. "You should keep your foot forward. Then the toes of both feet are in line with the pitch. Isn't that right, Lefty?"

"That's right," Lefty said. "People who put their foot in the bucket are usually ball shy. They want to be all set to duck away. And they are inclined to duck away too soon. Look, I'll show you."

Lefty placed Ken's feet so they were in a direct line with an imaginary pitcher's box. It seemed a little awkward. Ken kept wanting to drop the forward foot back, but, when he took a couple of practice swings with a make-believe bat, he could feel the improved balance and added power.

"Better?" Lefty asked.

"I think so," Ken said. Yet he wondered how it would be if he were standing up to a real plate with a pitcher actually chucking balls his way.

Amos seemed to have the same idea. "Lefty," he said, "why don't you pitch some balls to Ken?"

Lefty hesitated, then said, "I'd rather not pitch."

"It wouldn't really be pitching, Lefty," Ken said. "It would be helping."

Lefty smiled. "When you put it that way," he said, "it doesn't leave me much choice. After all, I am the Red Sox coach. I guess it's my job to help."

"I'll catch," Amos volunteered.

"With that glove?" Ken asked. "You'll think you're catching a swarm of hornets if you try to catch Lefty's pitches with a fielder's glove."

"It just happens," Lefty said, "that I have a complete catcher's outfit in the house. Mask, mitt, shin guards, and all. Dad got it when he used to practice with me. Wait a second, and I'll go get the stuff. Get my own glove, too. Think I've got a light fungo bat which should be about the right weight." He seemed almost eager as he went to get the equipment.

When Lefty returned, he got a white feed sack. He folded it to about the size of home plate. He placed it about ten feet out from the side wall of the barn.

"At least I won't have to chase the balls far if I miss them," Amos said. The mask, chest protector, and shin guards were big for Amos, but the protection was there just the same. That was what really counted.

Lefty paced off forty-four feet, which was regulation Little League distance from the plate to the pitcher's mound. He drew a line in the dirt with his toe.

"Don't bother to swing at them yet, Ken," Lefty said. "Just stand there and watch them. But keep your position, unless you really think you might get hit. I'll try not to do that."

"I'm not worried about you, Lefty," Ken said.

Lefty warmed up easily, but even so, the pitches came in faster than any of the Little-Leaguers could throw them. And Lefty was so big and long-armed that he seemed right on top of the plate.

"How about it, Amos?" he asked after the first few pitches. "Hurting your hand?"

"Not much," Amos said.

"Put this in the palm of your mitt hand." Lefty dug a small piece of sponge rubber out of his pocket. "It will help."

Ken kept his eyes on each pitch. Each time he was tempted to back away from one, he gritted his teeth and kept his feet planted solidly in position. The pitches were coming in faster and faster. Yet, not one was dangerously close, and Ken was glad he had held his place.

"Good going, Ken," Lefty said finally. "Start swinging at them now. Never mind trying to hit. Just swing through and keep your eye on the ball. I might even slip you a curve now and then."

"You're awfully close, Lefty," Ken said. "You're mighty big for a Little-League pitcher."

"Guess you're right, at that," Lefty answered with a smile. "I'll move back. I'm not used to pitching at this close distance, anyway. Think you can still hold them, Amos?"

"Sure," Amos said happily. "Boy, this mitt has really got a swell pocket. Doesn't hurt, either. Not with this sponge in my hand."

Lefty moved back a few more paces and drew another line on the ground. "Regular big-league pitching distance is sixty feet and six inches," he said. "This ought to be fairly close to it."

Lefty kept pitching and Ken kept swinging. Lefty would tell him when he was going to throw a curve. Ken watched them closely. Several times they bent in sharply toward him, and he was tempted to jump back out of the

123

Lefty kept pitching and Ken kept swinging

way. Then Lefty's curve would straighten out over the plate, and Ken was mighty glad he hadn't jumped.

"Good boy," Lefty said on several occasions. "Now hit a few. If they get by me, Prince will shag them. That dog's a natural ballplayer."

Nearly an hour went by. The sound of the ball popping into the pocket of the catcher's mitt echoed across the farmyard. Occasionally there was the solid crack of the bat and the happy barking of a dog, as Prince loped after the hit ball.

And only once did Ken jump back away from the plate. He heard Lefty's shout of warning, and hit the dirt. When he got up, grinning weakly, he saw Lefty wiping his forehead. His hand seemed to be trembling a little.

"I think we've had enough for today," Lefty said. "You're doing swell, Ken."

"Can we do it again?" Ken asked anxiously.

"We'll see," Lefty said. He still seemed a little shaken from that one pitch. Yet it hadn't been a fast one, and Ken had had no trouble getting out of the way. He wondered why it should bother Lefty.

A few minutes later Ken and Amos said good-by to Lefty and started the hike back toward town. They had walked nearly home when Amos said, "Ken, did you notice anything about Lefty's pitching?"

"Notice?" Ken asked. "Notice what? All I noticed was that he could really whiz that ball in. And his curve—wow!"

"Did you notice that not once did he try to throw you a high inside curve?"

"I'm glad he didn't," Ken said. "That's just where I don't like them."

"It's just where Lefty doesn't like to pitch 'em, too," Amos said. "That's the pitch he has trouble with, remember? It's the pitch that put Johnny Logan in the hospital."

"Meaning what?" Ken asked.

"Meaning that maybe you got some good out of the practice today," Amos said, "but I wonder if Lefty did?"

CHAPTER NINE

The season moved along fast. It was a close race between all four of the teams. Nearing the end of the second round of play, the Red Sox were just one game behind the leading Billings Hardware Giants.

The Giants had beaten them the first time around. And, although it hadn't been the deciding factor of the game, Ken had been driven back away from the plate by two of Randy Simmons' pitches. Both had been high inside curves. The umpire called both of them strikes.

Ken had learned to keep his feet squared away to the plate. He was hitting better because of it. But he still couldn't seem to face Randy without the urge to back away from the big left-hander's pitches.

He still couldn't erase the memory of the broken jaw and of Randy's pitch that had caused it. Although the plastic batter's helmet completely protected his head and ears, Ken couldn't help but feel that his jaw stood out like a beacon for one of Randy's pitches.

Now the Red Sox were in the second game with the Giants. Ken had hoped that some other pitcher would be on the mound. But, as luck would have it, Randy's turn came up again. The fourth inning was just beginning. The Giants were leading by a score of 5 to 3. The Red Sox came to bat with defeat staring them in the face.

Sam Silvers led off with a sharp single between third and shortstop.

Then, with the count two balls and one strike on Bruno, the base coaches relayed the hit-and-run sign to both batter and base runner. Bruno had to swing, no matter where the pitch came. For, as soon as the ball reached the plate, Sam would be digging out for second.

The pitch was low, but Bruno swung. His bat hit on top of the ball. The grounder bounded high toward the pitcher. Sam streaked for second like a greased gazelle. Seeing that there was no chance of a force-out on second, Randy whirled and pegged to first. Bruno was out by a step.

"All right, Ken," Lefty said from the dugout. "A hit's what we need. Don't let Randy worry you with those high pitches."

Ken was determined not to. But Randy was also just as determined to keep him from getting a hit. And the Giants' left-handed pitcher had one advantage—he knew Ken's weakness.

The first pitch was high but not close. Ken kept his position at the plate and let it go for

Ken let it go for a called ball

a called ball. He swung hard on the second pitch—a fast ball around the knees. Next he took a cut at a change-up pitch, cut too soon, and fouled it into the left-field stands.

Randy's arm came up, whipped forward, and the ball rocketed toward Ken, high and curving in.

Ken tried desperately to hold his place at the plate. Unless the curve broke in sharply, he knew it couldn't possibly touch him. And Randy couldn't throw a very sharp curve. Yet, when the pitch was still ten feet from the plate, Ken suddenly jumped away.

Even though the umpire called it a ball, Ken felt the warm blush rise into his cheeks as he stepped back up to the batter's rubber. There was no reason for jumping away from that pitch. No reason, at least, in the eyes of the people in the stands.

"Stick up there," someone yelled.

Ken was still rattled when Randy's next pitch came in. It was letter high, right over the center. Ken swung under it for the third strike. The catcher dropped the ball, but Little League rules didn't allow the batter to run for first on a dropped third strike. Ken went to the bench.

Al Archer, pitching that day for the Red Sox, popped a fly to short center to retire the side.

The Giants still led, 5 to 3.

The Giants got one more run in the bottom of the fifth inning. Amos hit a home run in the top half of the sixth to make the score 6 to 4 in favor of the Giants.

And that was how the game ended. The victory put the Giants two full games in the lead. The Red Sox were tied with the Pirates for second place.

If any of the players had noticed how Ken backed away from Randy's pitch in the fourth inning, no one mentioned it. Besides, he had made several good plays on the field and had scored one of the Red Sox runs. There were few players who had neither made an error nor fanned out that day. Randy Simmons was rated as the league's top pitcher. He had done well to prove it in the victory just finished.

Ken's father came out of the stands as the players began gathering up their equipment. "I only caught the last three innings, Ken," he said, "but it was a good game, what I saw of it."

"We lost, though," Ken said simply. He was pleased that his father had seen him play. But he also wondered if his father had noticed that one high inside pitch that he had backed away from.

"You can't win them all," Mr. Douglas said. "Or does that sound too corny?"

"Well, we better win more than we have, Dad," Ken said. "A few more losses and we'll be plumb out of the race."

"I suppose so," his father said thoughtfully. "Let's hope things get better. Well, I had to park over on Locust Street. Quite a crowd at these games, isn't there? Should be, too. It's good baseball. Any of you fellows want a ride home?" he called. "Bruno, you live out our way."

Bruno started to say something. Then he hesitated when he saw Amos standing beside Ken. "Thanks, anyway, Mr. Douglas," Bruno said, "but—well, I think I'll walk. Need the exercise. Helps keep me in shape, you know.

"It's up to you," Ken's father said.

"Come on, Amos," Ken invited.

"I can walk, Ken," the dark-skinned third baseman said. "Besides, it's out of your way to my place."

"I've got a tank full of gas, Amos," Mr. Douglas said. "Might as well let us drop you off."

"Come on, you goof," Ken insisted, tugging at his friend's arm. "Or do we have to fight?"

"I don't want any fights, Ken," Amos said, grinning. "Especially not with you."

The three of them started toward the car. Ken couldn't tell whether Amos was pleased to be coming along, or whether he was sad over something else which had just happened.

It was a cinch that Bruno had come up with a pretty flimsy excuse for not riding with them.

CHAPTER TEN

Ken lay awake thinking quite a while that night. There had to be some way to break himself of the fear of those high inside pitches. He had been doing pretty well on everything else. His fielding had improved steadily under Lefty's patient coaching. His batting average was climbing toward .300.

Yet, that one weakness was robbing him of his best efforts, both for himself and for the team.

It was like with Lefty. That one weakness of Lefty's was also keeping the tall southpaw from being a real big-leaguer.

Ken didn't realize it, but, as he finally dozed off, an idea had started to work its way into the corners of his mind.

When he awoke, with the sun just starting to pry in under the window shade, the idea was there, full grown now and demanding action.

It wasn't until nearly ten o'clock that Ken could get away. The hedge needed trimming first. His collection of stuff in the garage—stuff which his father sometimes impatiently referred to as junk—was crowding out the family car.

But by ten o'clock he had the hedge trimmed, and his treasures were neatly stacked in one corner of the garage. He even got rid of a couple of wooden crates which he had been saving to use for a soapbox racer. He might get at the job of building a racer next year. If so, he figured he could locate more crates when he really needed them.

After his mother's inspection of the chores, Ken got his glove and went to see Amos.

He nearly had to fight his way through the eight young Jackson children who were home. They were cute kids, every one of them. The Jacksons' home was not large, but it was neat and clean, both inside and out.

Amos was just finishing mopping the kitchen floor as Mrs. Jackson led Ken inside. She was quite heavy, but a very cheerful woman. Ken could see at once where Amos got his happy smile.

"Can you go out to Lefty's with me?" Ken asked.

"Soon as I'm through here," Amos said. "Just be a jiffy. What's up? You want Lefty to toss some more pitches at you?"

"Yeah."

"You don't seem to need it any more, Ken," Amos said. "You've been doing all right at the plate lately. At least," he added, "most of the time."

"Yeah, that's right," Ken said. "Most of the time. I want it to be all of the time."

"O.K., we'll go out," Amos said. He dipped

the mop in a pail of clean water, wrung it out, and made the final sweeps across the sparkling linoleum.

A while later, when they arrived at the farm, Ken and Amos found Lefty and his father out beside the barn changing a tractor tire.

"Well, you fellows are getting to be regulars out here, aren't you?" Mr. Gregory said. "Guess I'll have to teach you how to use a pitchfork."

"Lefty's been helping us," Ken said.

"We don't want to be nuisances," Amos said.

"Not at all. Not at all," Mr. Gregory assured them. "I'm a baseball fan, you know. Have been seeing a few of the Little League games, too. You come out any time you can. Might do Lefty a little good to handle a baseball once in a while himself."

Ken had the feeling that Mr. Gregory didn't entirely approve of Lefty having dropped out of big-league baseball.

"What's new, fellows?" Lefty asked.

"We thought maybe we could get you to pitch some balls to me, Lefty," Ken said.

"We've done quite a bit of that, Ken," the pitcher said.

"You saw what happened yesterday," Ken reminded him. He knew full well that Lefty hadn't missed his jumping away from the plate that one time. "Maybe just a little more and I'd have the thing really whipped. Really whipped for good—even against Randy Simmons."

"But if you're real busy, Lefty," Amos said, "well, we don't want to keep you from. . . ."

"Lefty's not busy," Mr. Gregory put in. "This tire is all set, except for putting a little wind in it. You go ahead, Lefty. Give the boys a hand."

Lefty got his glove, the catcher's gear for Amos, and the light bat. They didn't have to mark off the place beside the barn. Both the batter's box and the pitcher's mound were well worn where they had practiced before.

Lefty lobbed in a few easy pitches which Ken hit right back to him. Then, as Lefty's arm began to warm up, his pitches came in harder. Ken was no longer able to place his hits where he wanted them. It wasn't long until Lefty's dog Prince was tired out and panting from chasing the balls that swooshed past Lefty.

"Looks to me as though you fellows could use a fielder," Mr. Gregory said, coming out of the barn. "Mind if I use your glove, Amos?"

"Sure, you use it all you want, Mr. Gregory," Amos said. "This catcher's mitt is all I need."

"All right, Ken," Mr. Gregory said as he went out beyond Lefty. "Hit 'em out here. I used to be quite a ball hawk when I played for the Wheat Center Cougars." He laughed.

Ken hit a few, which Mr. Gregory caught with surprising ease. But Lefty had been pitching right where Ken liked them most—not where he needed them.

"How about giving me some to my weak

spot, Lefty?" Ken asked. "You know, high and inside."

The big pitcher paused and looked at Ken. "I—I'd just as soon not," he said.

"Please, Lefty," Ken said. "High and inside. That's where I need them. That's my weak spot."

"I know, Ken, I know," Lefty said. "But— well, it's my weak spot, too. I'd just rather not pitch them there, that's all."

"But I'll get out of the way, Lefty," Ken protested. "I'm not crazy enough to stand there and let myself get hit. No matter how important it is to square off to the plate, I'm not going to stay there and get hit by inside pitches. Go ahead. Try it, Lefty."

"Nope," Lefty insisted.

"Son," Mr. Gregory called, "if Ken isn't afraid, then go ahead. Give it a try."

"I'm not afraid, Lefty." Ken tried to sound more sure of himself then he actually felt. "Let 'em come. High and inside."

Lefty turned and stared away across the pasture for a minute. No one said a word to break whatever thoughts were going through his mind. It seemed to Ken that Lefty's face was more tense than it had ever been before. He saw the fingers of the pitcher's left hand tighten into a fist. Then they relaxed, and Lefty turned back toward the feed-sack home plate.

"All right, Ken," he said slowly. "We'll try a few."

"Attaboy, Lefty," Amos called. "Right here to me. Chuck 'em right in here." Amos held the mitt up high to give the left-handed pitcher a good target.

Lefty wound up gracefully. The pitch came in—fast, high, and inside. Ken never took his eyes off it from the very moment the ball left the pitcher's hand. He wasn't concerned with hitting it. He just wanted to be sure not to jump back unless he absolutely had to.

The pitch whizzed past. It wasn't much more than a foot from his face, but Ken held his ground. As the ball plopped into Amos' waiting mitt, he knew that there had been plenty of room to spare. He also knew that a month ago that same pitch would have had him flopping back to the ground to get out of the way.

"Ball one!" Ken cried happily. "Want to try for two, Lefty?"

The pitcher smiled thinly. The next one came in a little lower, a little closer. Ken took his short stride and swung. He barely ticked the ball. It bounced off Amos' mask and thumped loudly against the barn.

"Lefty," Amos called, "hook that curve in here. I think I can handle it all right."

"Take it easy, Amos," Ken cautioned over his shoulder.

"You started it," Amos said with a grin. "I want some fun, too. This catching behind the plate is really something. Don't know why I ever picked third base."

"All right," Lefty said. "I'll try one. You watch it, Ken. Watch it carefully. And don't stand up there if you think it's going to be too close."

The windup. The pitch started toward the

plate—fast, wide, and high. Then, about a third of the way out, it hooked sharply inward and downward. For a frightening moment, Ken thought it was going to curve in and hit him. He fought the temptation to jump back.

The ball hooked neatly over the inside corner for a cinch strike.

"That was a real lulu, Lefty," Amos cheered.

Lefty was grinning broadly. Ken had never seen him grin like that—really grin.

"Here's another one, Ken," he said. "Don't try to hit it. Just give me a few more practice tries."

The few practice tries lasted for nearly a half hour. When it was all over, Ken knew how it felt to be a sitting duck in a shooting gallery, yet not once had he gotten panicky and jumped back from the plate.

And not once had Lefty's pitches gone anyplace but where he had aimed them. The grin had never left Lefty's face. Except once. That was when he had stopped to laugh and to wipe something out of his eyes.

Now his face was shining with perspiration. It seemed to Ken that there was a little extra moisture in the big left-hander's eyes. But he was grinning, so Ken figured it couldn't very well be tears.

Lefty came up between the boys and put his arms around their shoulders. "That's it for today, fellows," he said. "Can't tire this wing of mine too much."

"Yeah, I'm a little tired, too, Lefty," Amos said.

"Me, too," Ken agreed. "But I think I've really got it whipped now, Lefty. What a day."

"What a day, indeed," Lefty said. "Just between you fellows and me, I think it's the greatest day of my life."

They couldn't quite figure what he meant by the remark. They were to find out—in time.

CHAPTER ELEVEN

The next week and a half were eventful days for the Brookdale Little League. The regular playing season was coming to a close. There were twelve Little Leagues in the district to which Brookdale belonged. Each League would have a winner. The twelve winners would play off for the district championship.

An aim at the district championship might lead all the way through the sectionals and to the regionals; might even end up with a trip to Williamsport as one of the eight teams in the Little League world series.

Right now every team was aiming sharply for the league championship—giving their all in the homestretch.

There had been plenty of upsets along the line. The Tigers had toppled the Giants with a surprising 8-to-3 victory. The Red Sox had nosed out the Pirates in an extra-inning game. But the Pirates had come right back and out-hit the strong Giants.

When the dust of the week and a half of games had settled, the Red Sox found themselves in a tie for first place with the Giants.

Today the grandstands were packed. People were even standing around the edge of the field. The final big game between the Red Sox and the Giants was about to begin.

The winner would be the Brookdale Little League champ. The winner would go on to the district play-offs.

This was the big game!

"Fellows," Lefty said after the pregame

warm up, "you have done great. Really swell. No one can take away from that no matter what happens this afternoon—win or lose. But, of course, let's win."

"We'll win, coach," Bruno promised boldly.

"If we don't," Ziggy said, "it won't be because we haven't tried."

"That's the spirit," Lefty said. "Now, we'll use the same line-up that we've used most of the season. It seems to click. There is only one small change. Ken, you bat in fifth place today. After Corky. Slats will come up after Bruno."

Ken felt a sudden thrill of pleasure surge through him. Being moved up from eight to fifth place in the batting order could mean but one thing. Lefty must consider him greatly improved as a hitter.

The score sheets of the past few games were proof of it. Ken was now batting a percentage of .326—a good batting average in any league.

"Grant," Lefty went on, "you're the starting pitcher. Al, you and Larry keep your arms warmed up. We can't take any chances on this one. All right, fellows, that's it. Stay loose out there. Back up your men. You outfielders stick to every play. Don't be caught flat-footed when there's a loose ball. Let's have plenty of chatter. O.K., shake hands and come out fighting."

The Red Sox grinned at Lefty's use of the prize-fighting phrase.

"Just one more thing," Lefty added. "After the game, win or lose, the treats are on me down at the Sweet Shop."

"Hey, you're stealing my speech, Lefty," said Captain McGrath, who was standing near by. "That was going to be my offer."

"O.K.," Lefty said, smiling, "that makes it double treats, fellows."

"Hurrah!" they chorused. They had been taking it easy on the sweet stuff. It had been part of the training Lefty had set up for them. They knew it had helped their playing, yet it hadn't spoiled their appetites for the fancy dishes at the Sweet Shop.

The Red Sox were the home team. They would bat in the last half of each inning. During the infield throws, while Grant was warming up on the mound, Ken had a chance to glance around at the packed stands. He saw both his mother and father sitting along the left-field line. He was proud to think that his father would close the bakery just so he could see the big game.

Both of Amos' parents were there, also. At least six of Amos' brothers and sisters were with them. They were happily munching popcorn and gazing with pride at their brother on third base.

Mr. and Mrs. Gregory were in the stands. Seated between them was a man Ken had never seen before. He was neatly dressed in a tan summer suit. He wore a straw hat. Not many people wore straw hats around Brookdale.

The umpires walked onto the field amidst a chorus of boos from the stands. Ken smiled to himself. Those boos were all a part of baseball. They didn't mean a thing. The umpires were swell people, on or off the diamond.

"Play ball!" the strike umpire called, after dusting off the plate with his whisk broom.

A lull settled over the stands as Grant wound up for the first pitch of the game. He delivered. The Giant batter swung and missed.

The silence broke under an avalanche of sound. From that moment on to the final play of the game, the area around the Brookdale Little League ball park echoed with loud and constant noise.

The batter worked Grant into a three-ball, two-strike count. He smacked the next pitch for a sizzler to the left of the pitcher's mound. Ken raced to his right. He snagged the ball with a neat backhand catch. He whirled and rifled the throw to first. Slats stretched far out and scooped it out of the dirt.

One away.

A single and an error on Corky Richards' throw from right field put a runner on second. Grant fanned the next batter. Amos pulled down a line drive to retire the Giants in the first inning.

Then Ken saw what he had hoped wouldn't be, yet had prepared himself to accept. Randy Simmons went to the mound to pitch for the Giants. And Randy proceeded to put the Red Sox down in order—no runs, no hits, no errors.

"We'll get to him next inning, coach," Corky promised, as the Red Sox started back out to their positions on the field.

"O.K.," Lefty said, smiling, "but just don't let them get to us this inning."

Lefty's words were not purposely ignored, but there was no stopping the Giants in the top half of the second inning. The first batter lifted a lazy fly over Slats Eldred's head. Corky Richards came racing in. Slats went racing out. Both were yelling so loudly for the ball that neither could hear the other. They collided, and the ball dropped to the ground. Taking advantage of the mix-up, the runner sprinted on to second.

Neither Slats nor Corky bawled each other out. It had been one of those things. Such mix-ups happened even in big-league games.

The next Giant batter socked another looping fly into deep right field. There was no mix-up this time. Corky smothered it for the out. But the runner tagged up and raced to third after the catch. He slid in ahead of Corky's throw. Safe. One away.

The following batter hit a grounder toward shortstop. Brick Osborn moved over in front of it. He was set for a quick throw to home plate to cut off the runner.

Then misfortune struck in the form of a pebble. The ball hit the small stone and took a wild hop over Brick's shoulder. It bounded into left field. The run scored easily. The batter pulled up on first with a "pebble single."

"Let's get a double," Ken called. "Pitch to him, Grant. We'll take him. Amos to me to Slats."

But the plan never jelled. The next Giant

batter—and a real giant, at that, it seemed to Ken—laid into the second pitch. The bat cracked sharply against the stretched horsehide cover of the ball. The round dot was still rising in the blue sky as it went over the left-field fence. It had been one of the longest-hit balls of the entire season, and it was a two-run homer.

Although Grant fanned the next batter, the Giants took the field for the last half of the second inning holding onto a comfortable 3-to-o lead.

"Don't let it worry you too much, fellows," Lefty said. "Just enough to get some hits. The game is still young."

Corky led off. He was small and hard to pitch to. He waited out the pitcher and got a free base on balls.

Ken stepped out of the "on-deck" circle and walked to the plate.

"Here's the easy one, Randy," the Giants' catcher jeered. "You know where he likes them."

Randy knew, and he pitched them there. But he pitched them too high and too close. Ken waited them out. He pushed back all temptation to jump back from the pitches. Both were called balls.

Randy was behind now. He had to pitch a good one. Ken looked to see if the bunt sign was on. It wasn't. Evidently, needing at least three runs, Lefty had decided to let them play an open game. No bunts.

True to Ken's guess, Randy's next pitch fairly floated in toward the plate. Ken slashed it into center field for a stand-up double. Corky went to third. No outs. It was a nice spot for the Red Sox. The fans in the stands were chanting it up.

Sam Silvers worked up a two-and-two count, then went out on a foul tip.

Bruno stepped up and got hold of a high pitch, slicing a long fly ball into right field. Corky tagged up and sprinted home after the catch.

Ken also tagged up. But he was an instant

late in getting away after the catch. The second baseman relayed the right fielder's peg to third. Ken was tagged out sliding into the base.

The score going into the third inning was Giants 3, Red Sox 1.

The third inning went scoreless for both teams.

Both teams added a run in the fourth. It was Giants 4, Red Sox 2, going into the fifth inning.

Grant had fanned two batters, and allowed seven hits. Only some smart and skillful fielding on the part of his teammates had kept the hits and the score down as low as they were.

Lefty thought it might be a good time to put Al Archer on the mound. Al had a rifle arm, but he was weak on curves. He was usually good for about three innings. There were only two innings left in the game.

Al walked the first batter. Bruno called time out and strode to the pitcher's mound. This was a poor time to be giving a free base

Bruno strode to the pitcher's mound

on balls. Ken trotted in to join the conference on the mound.

Bruno was saying, "You got it out of your system now, Al?"

"Yeah," the new pitcher said, "I think so, Bruno."

"Then let's get the next three batters," the Red Sox catcher said. He was smiling and he slapped Al on the pants before going back behind the plate.

Al seemed suddenly calmer. Ken admired the way Bruno could settle down a pitcher with just a moment's pause and a few helpful words.

"If you don't fan 'em, we'll take 'em, Al," Ken said, then trotted back to his position at second.

Al whizzed two pitches past the left-handed hitter. One was a ball, one a strike. The batter struck late at the next pitch. The ball bounded toward third base. Amos rushed in and took it on the big hop. Without pausing, he

159

whipped an underhand throw to Ken. Ken scuffed the bag with his toe. In full stride he leaped high to avoid the sliding runner's feet. Still in mid-air, he pegged to first. It wasn't a good throw; there hadn't been time for much accuracy. But Slats Eldred covered a lot of territory. He stretched far out and scooped the ball out of the dirt just before the runner's foot came down on the bag.

It was as neat a double play as had been made all season. The crowd roared its delight. Here was a brand of baseball they had hardly expected to find among players of Little League age.

Al Archer helped express his joy at getting out of the hole by fanning the next batter, to retire the side.

The Red Sox came in to bat. Randy Simmons didn't seem to have weakened any out on the mound for the Giants. With a two-run lead, and knowing he had only six more Red Sox batters to retire, he really bore down.

Bruno was first up. He slammed the second pitch straight back toward the pitcher's mound. It was too hot for Randy Simmons to handle. The ball glanced off his glove. Before the shortstop could chase it and get his throw away, Bruno was on first with an infield single.

With just two runs behind and no outs, Lefty again called for the sacrifice. Slats waited out two pitches, then bunted the ball neatly down the third-base line. The baseman ran in and scooped it up with his bare hand. He saw at once that there was no play at second. He whipped the ball underhand to first.

The throw was high. The first baseman leaped way up to get it. He came back down on the bag just in time to get Slats out. But, as the Giant first baseman was trying to regain his balance after the leap, Bruno rounded second and kept right on going for third. It was a nervy thing to do—wouldn't work once in a hundred times.

But Bruno wasn't afraid to take a chance. So surprised were the Giants that the Red Sox catcher was sliding safely into third under the first baseman's frantic throw before most people realized what was happening.

Then the crowd roared its approval of the heads-up ball playing. No base had ever been stolen more neatly.

One out and a runner on third.

Al Archer looked to see if Lefty was going to send in a pinch hitter. Lefty made no move, so Al stepped up to the plate. He choked up about three inches on the bat and swung into the first pitch. The ball sailed high, but short. The Giant second baseman backed up and took it. Bruno held third.

Two away.

Brick Osborn came up. He waggled his bat threateningly. He was determined to bring Bruno in.

But Bruno was doing some thinking of his own. He appeared very confident after his successful exhibition of base stealing. He kept one foot on the base, as was the Little League rule until each pitch crossed the plate. Bruno was poised like a sprinter ready to take off on a hundred-yard dash, although it was only sixty feet to home plate.

Then, on the third pitch Bruno saw his chance. The low curve got away from the Giants' catcher. Bruno made his break for home plate. He was running for all he was worth. The catcher scrambled for the ball which had dribbled a few feet behind him. Randy Simmons tore in from the mound to cover the plate.

The catcher located the loose ball and flipped it to Randy just as Bruno started his slide. It was a perfect toss from the catcher. Randy shoved down his glove just as Bruno's foot was reaching for the plate.

"You're out!" the umpire bellowed.

There was no arguing. It had been a good chance, and it had been close, but Bruno was out; barely, perhaps, but out just the same. A close out counted just as much against the team as being out by a mile.

The fifth inning was over. It was still Giants 4, Red Sox 2.

The Giants came to bat for their sixth and last time.

Al Archer fanned the first batter. The second man up popped out to Amos. It looked as though the Giants were going down in order.

Then something went wrong. Al grooved a pitch to the Giants' ace hitter. He pickled it for a two-bagger. Rattled, Al walked the next batter. Bruno called time out and strode to the mound. He talked to Al a moment. He seemed to be watching the pitcher closely.

"How about it, Al?" Bruno asked. "Think you can get the next man? It's important, pal."

"I—I don't know, Bruno," Al said, wiping away the sweat that had popped out on his forehead.

"You've been doing all right, fella," Bruno said. "But maybe you better rest. O.K.?"

164

"Maybe so, Bruno," Al said. "I'm not much of a pitcher when the heat's on. Someone else can probably do better."

The Red Sox catcher looked over at Lefty. Lefty made a sign toward the bull pen. Larry Smith walked slowly out to the mound.

"Put out the fire, Larry," Al pleaded, handing the ball to the new pitcher.

Larry took his five warm-up pitches. He motioned to the umpire that he was ready. He checked the runners on first and second.

Then, with amazing calmness, Larry proceeded to put out the fire. It took four pitches —one ball and three strikes.

Larry received a roaring cheer from the crowd as the Red Sox went in for the final turn at bat.

"That was as neat a piece of relief pitching as I've seen for a long time, Larry." Lefty patted the grinning boy's shoulder. "I guess there's no point in my telling you fellows that it's now or never. Anyway, as far as this season is concerned. Just be in there trying all of the time. The game's not over. Not by a long shot. Get those frowns off your faces."

The Red Sox tried to push smiles onto their faces. It wasn't easy. They had all been thinking exactly what Lefty had just finished saying.

It was now or never.

CHAPTER TWELVE

The top of the Red Sox batting order was up. Brick Osborn took plenty of time picking out his favorite bat, although there were only six to choose from.

"Start it out, Brick," Ziggy Ross encouraged from the batter's circle. "We'll bring you around."

"Oh, yeah," the Giants' catcher jeered. "You bring him around to mow the infield next week. We Giants are going to need it for the district play-offs."

Sensing victory, the Giants were chattering it up like a cage of monkeys.

Brick paid no attention as he stepped into the batter's box.

He took the first pitch for a called strike. The next one was a little low. Brick started to swing but held up. Ball one, strike one.

Randy Simmons wound up and threw. The ball started out wide. Nearing the plate, it began to curve in. Brick waited and watched. Judging the curve, he swung. There was the solid crack of hard leather on ash. The ball lined straight over the pitcher's head. Brick rounded first, but he scampered back as the center fielder scooped up the ball and pegged it to second. It was a clean single. Brick's face was wreathed in a king-size smile.

The crowd was on its feet. Some were shouting for a rally. Some were shouting just as loud to stop a rally. It all depended on which side they were rooting for.

"Keep it going, Ziggy," Bruno pleaded.

Ziggy tried, but he was overanxious. He swung at a bad pitch, and swung late. The ball dribbled between first and second. The keystone sacker spurted over and whipped the ball to the shortstop covering second. The shortstop tagged the bag and relayed the ball to first.

Only Ziggy's speedy legs kept him from being the victim of a fast double play.

With one out and Ziggy on first, Amos came to bat.

"Come on, Amos, boy," Bruno yelled. "We're all with you."

Amos backed out of the box and bent down to rub some dirt on his hands. Ken had a pretty good idea it wasn't the only reason Amos hesitated.

As far as he could remember, it was the first time that Bruno ever had shown Amos any kindness. Ken couldn't help but glance at Bruno. Bruno saw him and smiled. There was a little apology in the smile. There was a lot of

169

understanding. Bruno seemed to realize that the whole team had a single problem and a single goal. Nothing else mattered—least of all the color of a teammate's skin.

The whole team was cheering Amos on. Corky was the loudest, and Grant was next.

Amos' shoulders seemed even straighter than usual. He hit a two-and-two pitch for a scorching grounder. The third baseman knocked it down. But he couldn't get his hands on it to make a throw.

The scoreboard rated it as a single. Ziggy had sprinted to second. Amos was on first. One out.

The roar of the crowd was deafening.

Then Corky stepped up and hit the third pitch. Another cheer went up from the stands as the ball sailed high and far into right field. But part of the cheer turned to a groan, as the fielder ran back and made a beautiful catch over his shoulder. Ziggy tagged up and went to third after the catch. Amos was held on first.

Two outs.

"Well, Ken," Sam Silvers said, stepping into the batter's circle as Ken stepped out toward the plate. "It's up to you, fellow."

Just before reaching the plate, Ken paused and glanced back into the dugout. Lefty sat there smiling. He held up his hand, touching the tips of his thumb and first finger. "Good luck," the sign was saying.

But Ken knew that even if he fanned out, Lefty's smile would still be there. It was comforting to know.

Randy Simmons smiled as Ken squared away at the plate. Randy had failed to make him back up the other two times Ken had been at bat, yet Ken had the feeling that Randy hadn't given up trying.

"Here's our pigeon," the Giants' catcher shouted. "The game's practically over now. Feed 'em to him, Randy."

"Don't let him bother you, Ken," Amos called from first base. "Murder that apple, Ken. Remember what we've been doing."

Ken remembered, all right. He was remembering with all his might.

Ken was expecting Randy's first pitch to be high and inside. But Randy fooled him with a straight speeder over the outside corner.

"Strike!" the umpire called.

"Two more, Randy," the catcher yelled. "Just two more."

Randy checked the runners from his set position on the mound. Then he reared back and whipped his left arm forward. The pitch rocketed in high and fast.

The ball had no more than left the pitcher's hand than Randy shouted. "Duck, Ken. Duck!"

It was no false alarm intended to rattle him. Randy was not that kind of guy. Besides, Ken could see the pitch coming. There was no curve to it. If there had been, it would be in the wrong direction.

Ken dropped his bat and hit the ground. The catcher barely got his mitt on the ball.

Randy Simmons walked halfway in to the

plate. "I'm sorry, Ken," he said. "I didn't mean it. The ball got away from me."

"It's O.K., Randy." Ken got up and started to brush himself off. He felt shaky.

"You all right, son?" the umpire asked. Ken wondered if fright showed on his face. He wondered if he had gone pale.

"Yes, sir," he said. "I'm O.K."

"One ball, one strike," the umpire reminded, holding up a finger of each hand.

Before stepping back into the box, Ken took another glance toward the dugout. Lefty was watching him closely. But the smile was still on the big-leaguer's lips. "When you need to duck, you need to duck," he called.

Ken took a deep breath. It helped to calm the butterflies inside his stomach.

The next pitch was where the first one had been. Hard and on the outside corner. Ken swung, but barely ticked it off the end of his bat.

One ball, two strikes. Randy was way ahead of him on the count.

The Giants' pitcher could afford to waste a pitch now. Ken knew that the one place Randy might figure to waste it, and still have a chance of fanning him, was high and inside.

It wasn't that Randy would be trying to brush him off. It was just a matter of good baseball to throw to a batter's weak spot.

It was even more than that when it could mean the championship.

"Watch out for this one," the catcher warned. Ken could take the remark to mean anything—or nothing. The Giants' catcher was a clever ballplayer. He seemed to know just how to rattle the batters.

The memories of the practice sessions out at the Gregorys' farm flashed through Ken's mind. He remembered how he had handled some of the high inside pitches which Lefty had become so skillful at serving up to the plate. He hadn't hit many of Lefty's pitches. But when he had, there was a little trick he had used to do it. Maybe Lefty had noticed it; maybe he hadn't.

Ken decided to try it now. If Randy crossed him up on the pitch, it would just be too bad.

But Randy didn't cross him up. As Randy's arm went back for the pitch, Ken shifted away from the plate just a couple of inches. That pitch just had to come over on the inside, he thought. He would never be able to reach a pitch over the outside corner. But that was the chance he had decided to take. He didn't believe Randy would be trying for the outside corner.

The pitch started toward him, high and outside. Outside! Then Ken saw that it was curving. It curved down and in. For a moment it appeared to be curving in too much toward him. Ken set himself firmly. He was determined not to jump back unless there was no other choice. But it was no wild pitch this time. Randy had put everything he had into it. The ball was hooking sharply toward Ken.

At the instant Ken saw that it was going to cross into the strike zone, he shifted his left foot forward in a short stride. He put all of his weight and muscle into the swing of the bat.

Although the pitch was close, Ken was prepared for it. The couple of inches he had shifted back were just enough to bring the fat part of the bat against the ball. Had he not shifted back, it would have hit on the handle.

The crack was almost like that of a .22 long

rifle. Ken felt the solid impact on the bat. He saw the ball begin to rise. He dropped the bat, ducked his head, and started running.

Everyone was running. Ziggy was tearing away from third base. Amos' legs were churning in the direction of second. It seemed suddenly that everyone was running and yelling. It wasn't until he had rounded second himself and was heading for third that Ken caught sight of the sad looks on some of the Giants'

faces. Then he saw the left fielder standing with his hands on his hips, staring beyond the left-field fence.

"Might as well slow down," the Giants' shortstop said. "Save your running for the district play-offs. You're a hero, Ken. What a home run!"

Ken loped on in behind Ziggy and Amos. The moment his foot touched the plate he was mobbed.

He was too happy to realize just what was happening. He felt himself being lifted up into the air. He saw the sea of shoulders beneath him. He barely noticed the flicker of photographers' flash bulbs in his face. He saw Lefty trying to get through the crowd. He caught a brief glimpse of his father and mother waving from the grandstand.

There were a hundred and one things happening. It was mass confusion, but wonderful.

Then he realized that some sort of a parade had formed. It started marching around the ball park.

Ken was still high up on a wave of bobbing shoulders.

He laughed, and settled back to enjoy the ride.

CHAPTER THIRTEEN

After the awards had been presented, the happy group of Red Sox started toward the Sweet Shop. Each boy proudly carried a small leather-covered jewel case with his individual medal inside. The championship cup, after it was engraved with the proper names and information, would be kept on prominent display at the firehouse. In coming years young boys would admire it. They would go out and try to win one just like it.

But, whether they won or lost, they would have fun trying. That was the best trophy of all.

Bruno said, "Boy, I feel like a five-star general with this medal. What's yours like, Amos?"

"I think they are all the same, Bruno," Amos said, smiling. He opened his own case and showed the medal to the Red Sox catcher.

"They're the same," Bruno said, nodding. "Just the same. And that's exactly the way it should be, huh?"

"That's the way it should be," Ken said.

Amos smiled happily. He knew what they meant.

Captain McGrath had gone on ahead of them. When the team walked into the Sweet Shop, every one of the players stopped and gasped. Streamers of red-and-white crepe paper hung all over the place. At one end of the room was a large bright banner. The one

182

word that smacked them right between the eyes was CHAMPIONS.

They let out a wild cheer and crowded to the tables, which were set and waiting.

Then Lefty came in and they cheered again. Corky started to sing "For He's a Jolly Good Fellow." The room fairly rocked as everyone joined in.

Ken noticed that the man in the tan summer suit and the straw hat was with Lefty.

Captain McGrath got up and said, " 'Fraid I'll have to withdraw my offer, fellows. Just a single treat today. But a big single treat. Don't want you to be getting out of shape for the district play-offs, you know. My treat will come along later. This one is on Lefty. And for good reason. Tell them all about it, coach."

Captain McGrath sat down. Lefty Gregory stood up. Ken had never seen Lefty look so happy as he did now.

"Fellows," he said, "you are the greatest team in the world. And I'm probably the proudest man in the world for having had the chance to work and play with you. I'm almost certain that you will cop the district championship. It wouldn't surprise me to see you go all the way to the Williamsport world series."

They cheered.

"I'm only sorry," Lefty went on, "that I won't be in the Red Sox dugout while you're doing it."

A sudden silence fell over the room.

"Fellows," Lefty said, "I'm happy and proud to tell you that I'm going back to the Cardinals."

Almost without realizing it, Ken was on his feet waving wildly and screeching at the top of his lungs. But he was only one of many.

Lefty stood quietly smiling. He looked from one player to another. He started to blink his eyes, and Ken saw a drop of moisture roll down along the side of his nose.

"Thanks, fellows," Lefty said after the uproar had quieted down. "Maybe you have been wondering about this gentleman with

184

me. Red Sox, I'd like to present Mr. Floyd Harkness, manager of the Cardinals. You probably know him as 'Jojo' Harkness, one of the all-time great major-league shortstops."

"Wow!" Bruno exclaimed. "Jojo Harkness!"

But his words were lost in another cheer.

"I'll be mighty brief," the Cardinal's manager said after the room had quieted down once again. "This is really your day. And a great day it is. I don't want to steal your thunder. But I will say that it is Lefty's day, also—and mine. We have needed Lefty on the Cardinals. I guess you know why he came home. Things like that happen, and no one is really to blame. It's one of those things. Tough. But there is no problem that can't be whipped."

Ken smiled to himself. His father had said the very same thing.

"But sometimes a fellow needs a little help," Mr. Harkness continued. "Lefty got that help, although he tells me that he wasn't very willing to accept it at first. He got it from

185

the team as a whole. He got it particularly from two fine Red Sox players—Amos Jackson and Ken Douglas."

The players looked at Ken and Amos. The team hadn't known about the practice sessions that had been going on out at the Gregory farm. Both Ken and Amos were blushing, although Ken's face was the only one which showed it.

Lefty got up again. He told the team the whole story. He told them about the first day. He told them about the last few days, and how Ken had finally coaxed him to start throwing the high inside curves which he so dreaded doing.

"I think Ken and Amos were more interested in helping me than they were in my helping them," Lefty said, "but I don't suppose you could get them to admit it. They had a faith in me that I didn't have in myself."

Ken started tracing imaginary pictures on the tablecloth with the handle of his spoon.

He had to do something to keep from bursting with good feelings.

"I am happy to tell you, also," Lefty continued, "that Johnny Logan, the—the man I accidentally beaned, is back on his feet and good as new. He will be playing with the Cards when I get back."

Another cheer.

"And that's about it," Lefty said. "Fellows, we've licked a lot of problems together this summer, haven't we?"

Ken nodded eagerly. He knew his own problem had been solved.

Amos was nodding, too, and grinning broadly. Amos had no problem. Not any more.

Everyone was happy as could be.

"Again," Lefty said, "thanks to all of you. You are all champions. Real champions. I hope to see you at the world series."

"Which world series, Lefty?" Bruno called. "Little League or major league?"

"Both," Lefty said.

They stood up and cheered again. Then they sat down. The dishes loaded high with ice cream and fancy sauces were being brought in.

And they were ready for them!

END